I0456559

DEDICATION

This story is dedicated to my grandmother, born Virginia Elizabeth Vieregge in 1919. As a young woman living in a small town in East Texas she dreamed of becoming a writer. She pulled together her best stories and all her courage and went to the local newspaper. It was customary for newspapers to print fictional work meant as entertainment segments. There, the editor and owner of the paper did not meet her with encouragement, but instead told her it was man's job, not for silly girls and she needed to run back home and tend the house like a woman should. He did not even look at her work. Living in that small town her entire life, her stories were never published and rarely seen by only the privileged few with whom she shared them. Despite, and perhaps because of her ill treatment, she always encouraged my writing endeavors. She is a large part of the inspiration of this series, depicting the trials of girls as they turn into women. Dreams are sometimes crushed, fought for, or even new ones realized in this age old struggle every woman has faced, in the years between the child we are taught to be and the women we choose to become. My grandmother is a large part of who I chose to be.

CONTENTS

ACKNOWLEDGMENTS

Thanks to my husband, Jake for his unrelenting support
and my dear friends.

CHAPTER ONE: 1898

Dearest Cousin Rachel,

I do hope this letter finds you and Uncle Theodore and
Auntie Mabel in good health and fortune. I adored your
last letter telling of the vast lands and huge skies of your
new home. I know you, Tildie and Auntie Mabel were so
glad to see your father again. I would truly love to hear
more about the steele rail cart ride there. How can you
sleep on such a thing? I believe it would make me ill to
move along at such a pace both day and night. Have you
seen any Mexicans in Texas? I hear tell there are many
there. What about cowboys and gunfighters? Are the
towns as perilous as they say? Oh, I do miss you so much.
If all is well there, perhaps Father will allow me to visit.

Father sent me to Lavelle's yesterday to be fitted in my
dress for Friday next. I only wish you were still here to
attend, but I will not miss a single detail in my next letter. I
cannot wait. Father has invited everyone, it will be as big as
my coming out party last year. Seventeen! I am sure it will
be exciting and my gown is to be beautiful. It is gold
brocade with ivory taffeta and fine Irish lace. I just wish

1

Mother were here to see it. I think that is why Father is so insistent about making my birthday special. It seems almost every family we know lost someone to the epidemic this year. It is not fair. Father wants me to smile and be happy. He always smiles and tries to look cheerful when he is home and we sit in the parlor, but when I come into the room, before he sees me, I look at him and he does not look cheerful at all. He looks so sad and old.

I still cry at night sometimes, though I do not tell Father. I do not wish to worry him more. I keep Mother's photograph beside my bed and talk to her sometimes. Is that foolish?

I am sorry. Here I am going on about sad things. That seems rather selfish, considering your loss last year. Some day there will be no more epidemics or influenza.

Better things, though. I was shopping last Tuesday and guess who I saw. It was Artie Rutherford, you know, Charles Rutherford's son. Well, as I walked pass, pretending not to notice him at all, he smiled at me and tipped his hat. I do not know exactly why, but something about the way he looked right at me made me blush all the way to my boots. I looked through the guest list on Father's desk, and his family has responded to their invitation, so he will be at the party. I keep wondering if he will ask me to dance. Father mentioned him a couple of weeks ago, also. Says that he is about to graduate from the university and Father is considering hiring him on at his firm. Father thinks he shows promise as a future legal mind. But I think I fancy his dark, wavy hair and green eyes.

Are there any decent gentlemen out there? I cannot imagine what it must be like to live so far away from town. But I am sure it is as beautiful as you say. I am enclosing an invitation to my party. I think they are lovely. I know, of course, that you cannot come, but I just could not stand not inviting my favorite cousin. We have been like sisters all our lives. Be sure to write back and tell me everything you discover. I know you had only just arrived in your last letter and it was so good to hear that you had made a safe journey of it. Give my love to Auntie Mabel, Uncle Theodore and little cousin Tildie. I hope to hear from you soon.

Love,
Maggie

12 May 1898

Dearest Cousin Rachel,

I was so excited to receive your letter yesterday. Those storms of dirt sound awful. I cannot imagine what it must be like. But otherwise everything seems wonderful. Is the ranch really that big?

Well, I have so much to tell you. Remember Artie? Ever since the party, which was magnificent, he has come to the parlor twice a week to visit, supervised by Nanna, of course. Artie has asked to accompany us to Church on Sunday and Father said yes. I think Father approves of him as a suitor. He is so nice. His hair has beautiful waves that end in slight curls dancing around his head. He is so intelligent and knows all of politics and laws and he talks to me. I mean, of course he talks to me when we sit in the parlor, but he does not just treat me like a silly girl. I never realized I had so many opinions! And even though some may be rather ridiculous, he still listens and does not laugh at me. It feels almost scandalous sometimes, as if he is looking into me. I still blush when he stares into my eyes. I do not think Nanna notices, but she does quite a bit of huffing when we discuss the policies of President McKinley, who Artie met only a few months ago.

I now wish I had cared more about Father's business and politics. I would feel more secure that I am not making a fool of myself every time I open my mouth. But it does feel so good that he finds my opinions are important. I hope he will ask to go walking soon. I have the perfect strolling dress picked out. It is a smart looking green with tailored bodice and gold double breasted buttons down the front. I think the color will match Artie's eyes! Do you suppose if we had children, would they have green or blue eyes? I should not say such things. It is not right to presume too much. Oh, I wonder if he will ask to escort me to the June Ball. I am sure Father would allow it.

Oh, I am sorry. I have gone on and on about Artie. I guess I am just so excited. You remember how Father treated Taylor Detfrey and Nathan Grant. Father said Taylor was of poor stock and that Nathan did not have a brain at all. Of course, he was probably right. Taylor married last month and you would not believe who. He married Esmeralda Pippin. And, when I was in Lavelle's last week, I heard she had already come in to be fitted for a family gown. Seems a bit quick, if you ask me. Not to mention they had no engagement at all. The whole wedding was a small affair with just their close family, over and done quick. My wedding will not be like that. I want to fill the Cathedral for my wedding.

So, you did not mention if you had met any suitors out there in the West. Do the men really carry guns slung about their waists? Are there really gun battles in the streets? Oh, what about Indians? Have you met any? Nanna says that Indian women are beautiful and they have some sort of magic that ensnares men to marry them. She says that right good men will leave their whole family and run off with Indian maids. But I haven't read anything like that myself and I do not know where Nanna hears such things. Oh, maybe Father will let me visit once you are well settled.

I promised to tell you all about my party. It was divine. There must have been more than a hundred guests arrive and Father had the symphony perform. We ate roasted duck on beautiful ecru china. Father led me in the first waltz and told me I looked as beautiful as my mother. My eyes started to burn when he said that. I do wish Mother could have been there. I had to dab my eyes quick. I did not want to tearstain the light rouge I wore for the evening. Artie did ask me to dance and I danced with him several times throughout the night. In fact, he stayed very near me most of the evening and his brother Jonathan even scolded him for not sharing me with my other guests. Dancing with Artie was like floating across the floor. I think I would have been happy if he were the only guest to show up! He wore a smart black coat and he kissed my hand when he came through the reception line. And I mean he actually kissed it! I felt like I had swallowed a bee that was just buzzing around, all through my insides. I do not think I will ever forget his warm breath against my skin. Oh, now, Rebecca. You must promise never to show this letter to anyone, ever! If Father ever heard me say such a thing he would indeed be quite upset and I would not want to be thought of as a harlot, either! I know I can trust you, it is just writing something like that down and it looking you right back in the face seems a bit more startling than whispering in our garden. Oh I wish you were still here. There is just so much to say and tell, it swims all through my head and I know I cannot just write on and on forever.

I must say that Father is doing quite well. He seems a bit happier lately. I am not sure why, if it is my courtship with Artie because he talks about it frequently. Cousin Elaine is excited. She is planning her coming out party for September. Poor thing. She is so sweet. I do hope it all goes well for her. I think her family is having some difficulties. I overheard, by accident of course, Uncle Frederick speaking with Father in the library and Uncle Frederick was asking Father for a loan. So when I hear Elaine talk about all the costly things she wants, I hope their family will be able to afford it. I would hate to see her disappointed.

Well, I hope this letter has found you in good health and spirits. I cannot wait to hear from you again. I want to hear all about everything. Please write soon. Give the family my love.

Love,
Maggie

5 July 1898

Dearest Rachel,

I hope all is better out there. I am so sorry to hear you are unhappy. Perhaps Uncle Theodore would let you come and visit for a while. I am sure Father would be more than happy for you to come on an extended visit. I really thought you moving west would be a great adventure and you were always so much more daring than I. But I guess it would be rather lonely moving from the city to a place like that. I thought the nearby town would be something like here or at least like Benchwater. I cannot even imagine having to make a full day's ride just to buy a corset or some lace. You know what, Lovelle's has some beautiful Irish lace in right now. I was just admiring it yesterday. I will send some to you. I am sure you can make good use of it. You are so fine at sewing.

Well, Uncle Theodore will just have to let you come and visit, anyway. I have news I am busting to tell and was about to write to you anyway before I received your letter. I am so excited and happy and scared! Artie asked me to marry him three days ago. Of course, father knew it was coming. Artie had already discussed it with him. And Father, what a scoundrel, he did not say a word of it to me. We arranged for tea in the garden. Well, I knew Artie would be coming, but still, I had no idea. Thinking back, I should have known. Father had sent me downtown to buy a new dress and hat last week and then that morning he suggested I wear it.

We were sitting and having tea and biscuits and Father and Artie were discussing something from work. Artie has now joined Father's firm. I was sitting there thinking. Actually, I was thinking there just might be too many feathers in my new hat and wondering if I looked like an ostrich, when Father stood up and said he would leave us in private for a few moments. Of course, I was shocked. I mean, you know how old fashioned Father is about things like that. He has never allowed unsupervised courting. I was so shocked it took a moment for me to realize that Artie was asking me to walk with him through the garden. He took my hand in his and we walked the rose path. I felt utterly alone with him and thought I would faint. I mean, what if he wanted to kiss me? What would I do? I mean, not the little kiss on the cheek, but a real kiss. So we were standing there amid the flowers and I was thinking about all this when he turned full to me and held both of my hands in his grip. His hands are so strong and mine seemed small in comparison. I felt like a little girl. I looked up at him and he was smiling and he drew this large breath and I thought for sure, that was it. He was going to kiss me and there was no way I would be able to deny him. But instead, he said, "Margaret Florence Baine, would you do me the honor of becoming my wife?"

Well, my mouth fell open before I could stop it and I am sure I looked rather silly, but I did find a way through all my shock to say, "Yes." Then he drew from his coat an incredible sapphire ring. It is so beautiful. And then, he kissed me. The kiss. And I did not feel like a harlot at all. It was pure happiness and love. We always wondered what it would be like and now I just cannot find the words to describe it. When we came again to the sitting area, father had already returned and was smiling as big as I have ever seen.

So, you see, Uncle Theodore must let you come to visit, as I need you to be my maid of honor and help me plan the most extravagant wedding that Father can afford!

It will be so much fun.

You must write me back as soon as you can and let me know when you will arrive. I cannot wait to see you. I hope this news cheers you. Oh, and Jonathan is available still, only five years our senior and quite handsome, himself. He asked about you just yesterday at the Independence Day Lunch at Church. That would be wonderful, if we married brothers. Then we really could be sisters! Oh, I know. That is looking too far off, but I am so excited I just want you to share this with me, too.

The June Ball was lovely this year. It seemed different with an escort. I felt more grown up. Father escorted Mrs. Connors. Her husband passed away last year, thrown from a new horse. She has two sons, nine and eleven. She and Father seemed quite acquainted and I did not realize they knew each other that well. I thought it looked rather odd, seeing them together. She is a bit heavy if you ask me and not nearly as pretty as Mother. But I do want him to be happy. I did see him smiling and laughing more than usual. In fact, he really has seemed happier lately. I wonder now. Before I thought he was just happy about Artie and me, but perhaps there is more to it. Do you think he could be courting Mrs. Connors? Well, I will let you know if I find out anything more and you write me back as soon as you get this and tell me when you can come. I hope to hear from you soon and give all the family my love.

Love,
Maggie

30, August 1898

Dearest Rachel,

Well, this just will not do at all. I cannot believe Uncle Theodore is so set and stubborn. I do not care where you move to, we are family and I would expect the journey for my wedding, anyway. Why, you know I would travel around the Earth for you. I will tell Father and see if he can persuade him. I cannot imagine what kind of trouble he thinks you could possibly cause. We want you here. That is all Father has heard me talk about, "When Rachel gets here we will start planning at once!" I must have said it a hundred times since I sent my last letter. I have not started a thing, just waiting on news from you. My heart half hoped that by the time I received your letter you would already be on your way. I will ask Father. Surely Uncle Theodore will allow it if Father insists. But this delay means that I may need to begin planning before you arrive. The inscriptionists require at least six months to complete the invitations and we must decide on the stationary, ink, script and seals before they can even start. And I must send them out two months before the wedding. Artie has family far away and their post is slow. We did set the date. We will be married on 2 July, 1899, exactly one year to date from Artie's proposal. That is what Mother and Father did and I think it is sweet.

Father wishes to have our engagement party in the first part of October, but it will be hosted by the Rutherford's estate. I am to meet with Artie's mother next week to discuss those details. I feel nervous about it. They are quite nice, but I think they find me childish and not sophisticated enough. Their family is so political and important, though I know they hold Father in high esteem. My brief discussions with Artie's mother tell why he so openly discusses worldly affairs with me. She is astounding. She is as fluent with government as Father is. She even insists that women will be voting and holding office soon. I am not sure I want that responsibility. She seems so progressive and I cannot help but remember Mother in comparison. Mother did not care about such things at all and would fan her hands, as if clearing the air, when Father began going on. She did not want all those worries infesting her tranquil home. Father loved that about her. What is so wrong with being a wife and a mother? I hope Artie does not expect so much from me! But I do love him, and I expect I will be whatever he requires. I think I could find a comfortable place somewhere between the two. What do you think?

Times like this are when I miss Mother the most. She would so love to plan my wedding. But I believe I shall wear her gown. Father said I could have whatever I wanted made and to not even consider the cost, but I told him that I would like to wear Mother's and I saw tears fill up in his eyes and he said that would be just fine. I will have it brought out tomorrow so we can see what shape it is in. However, the attendants' gowns must be decided on and I will look to you for much help there. I want you to be beautiful, too. Not like Frederica's wedding. Oh those were terrible, weren't they?

You sounded so miserable in your letter. I wish I could do something to help. Have you been ill? Your letter sounded tired and near frail. You must stay well so that you can come. But if you are ill, perhaps you should come anyway and see a real doctor. I had better end here. I feel I could go on writing forever and never say everything in my head, but it would certainly take too long to read. I will ask Father to contact Uncle Theodore as soon as he comes home.

And that does remind me, I do believe Father has taken up with that Mrs. Connors. He is out into the early evening three days a week and she and her sons accompanied us to Church last week. I am not sure just yet how I feel about this. Perhaps it will fade and I will not have to worry with it. But I do not feel keen on the idea of having two little step brothers all of a sudden. Mr. Connors left them with an ample estate, but it is nothing like Father's and I am not sure just what would be expected from him in raising those boys. Of course, he would see them educated, no doubt, but that aside, Mrs. Connors is so much younger than father. I am just not sure I would want her as heiress to our estate. She appears nice enough, but something deeper does not seem right. You know she did not come from here, but says she moved here as a teenager to help a sick aunt. Mrs. Tanner, in Lavelle's, said that Mrs. Connors came from nothing, and that her parents were poor and lived in a mud house. Said she had naught but the dirty clothes on her back when she arrived here. If it were not for Mrs. Pinion, her aunt on her mother's side, she would still have nothing. Mrs. Pinion cleaned her, trained her and dressed her up, then found a good stationed husband for her. Sounds like she came to receive some help rather than give it. But who knows what the truth really is. Perhaps she did come to help her aunt and then was rewarded nicely for it.

Well, once again I have continued to rattle on and on. I do hope we can get everything situated. I look forward to hearing from you. Give my love to all the family.

Love,
Maggie

15 October, 1898

My Dear Cousin Rachel,

I received your letter yesterday. It saddens my heart to think that you will not come, but even more that you have been so ill. I wish I knew more what is wrong or that I could help in some way. You must get well. Perhaps if you recover soon, you will be able to attend, at least. We will see. Send all your measurements and I will have a gown made ready, just in case. If you are still too frail to come, then I will send you the dress as a token of our love and a present for whom I would choose as my maid of honor. The prospect of a new dress always lifts my spirits, so much so that my father thinks it may be a cure for any ailment I acquire! I wish I could go out there and nurse you back to health, myself. Your letter sounds so desperate and sad. Surely not everything could be so terrible.

I have not been idle. In fact, I am almost overwhelmed with preparations. There is so much to decide. I am sure that Artie's mother would offer more assistance if I asked, but I am still less than comfortable with her. The engagement party is in a few days. I will enclose the invitation.

And speaking of preparations. Father knows I have been so busy with everything. He suggested that I might ask Mrs. Connors to help me, since Mother is not here. Can you believe that? As if she could, even by the smallest token, replace Mother. It does not sound promising at all. She accompanies us to Church every week, along with her two little boys. Though I do feel somewhat sorry for them. They seem lost and still mourn for their father. But I do not believe I care for Mrs. Connors one bit. I think she tries to undermine Father's affection towards me. I know that sounds silly and childish, but listen to this. Two weeks ago we were in the garden and Mrs. Connors was here for tea. I was discussing the engagement party when Father asked if I had gone to Lavelle's yet to fit for a new dress. Just as I was about to tell him, Mrs. Connors pipes up and says, "A new dress just for that. Surely she has plenty of dresses already. Isn't it a bit frivolous to spend so much on a wardrobe?"

Well, thankfully, Father was not enticed by her idea. He said that money was not meant to be hoarded and he could think of no better use for it than to adorn his little girl. Is that not lovely? It nearly brought tears to my eyes, but Mrs. Connors looked annoyed. I wanted to say some really mean and nasty things to her, but somehow, I think the sweet words father chose made a deeper impression than any insult could. Of course I had already long since chosen my pattern and fabric. I have never heard such, to wear something pulled out of the trunk. At least I know she does not have Father's ear. But I will not be asking her for help in my wedding. That is for certain. Would you?

Oh, Rachel, I miss you so much. I just want you to be

as happy as I am and I cannot stand it otherwise. Please be well soon or I fear I will be destined to postpone my wedding and come nurse you myself, just to make sure a proper job is done of it.

Please give all my love to the family. I hope to hear from you soon. Please write as often as you feel you can. It must be lonely in bed through the long hours of the day. When I write to you, I feel a glimpse of your companionship again. Sometimes it is the only way for me to sort through and put to order all the dramas dancing in my mind.

Please hurry to full recovery and then I may see you soon.

Love always,
Maggie

20 December, 1898

Dear Cousin Rachel,

Merry Christmas. I am so glad to hear that you are feeling better and able to sit at your desk for a while. Your recovery seems so slow, has the doctor determined your ailment yet? It seems strange to me, but most important, you are finally getting better. For that we are all thankful.

This will be our first Christmas apart and I miss you terribly. I feel torn between misery and joy. I miss you, all of you and Mother so much, but this is also my first Christmas betrothed to Artie. He gives me hope when I feel all alone inside. I guess he reminds me of Father in that respect.

And about Father! I over heard him speaking with Mrs. Connors in the parlor last week. You would not have believed it. And yes, I know it is impolite to eaves drop. Nanna would have had my skin on a rug beat if I had not caught her listening in first. Nanna seems to agree with my appraisal of Mrs. Connors. We both worry that Father could be enchanted by her, in part, out his loneliness and desperation to escape the grief of losing Mother. But she does not seem too grief stricken regarding her husband. Please do not tell Father I said this, I do not wish to hurt his feelings, but I think she is an opportunist looking to improve her station. She is still young enough to bare children, too. And that is what I think. I believe she wants to marry Father as soon as possible, give him a child. I am sure she is hoping for a son, and then have a legitimate claim to Father's estate and the respect that goes with it. I know I sound rash, but you did not hear them.

Mrs. Connors seemed to want to marry soon, but Father wanted to wait until after my wedding. She did not seem too agreeable and told Father that she felt I needed a mother figure to help her, that I was becoming spoiled and she feared I would expect such treatment from a new husband as well, saying young Mr. Rutherford may not be able to keep up. We did not hear Father make any remarks to these comments, but when she said I needed to learn some humility, he piped in with a big, "What?"

Can you believe this, she actually suggested to him that I work down at the hospital. This is the epidemic season! Father did lose his temper there. Certainly she must know that is how Mother died. In fact, that is almost what Father said. He informed Mrs. Connors that he would not allow, under any circumstances, for his daughter to step foot in that place and if she had any ideas otherwise, she could voice them in her own parlor to herself. And he told her that he felt I had learned too much of humility weeping over my mother's photograph. That actually surprised me. I was unaware he knew so much of my grief. But Father is quite intuitive, at least when it comes to me. Then she rounded back on getting married. It seems he has already asked her but is unwilling to announce it until after my marriage to Artie. When it became obvious he had set his mind, she changed her attitude quick and became loving and supportive. A little too quick, if you ask me. And by too quick, I mean less than genuine. She wants to marry him as swift as possible and I do not believe for one instant she has given up the battle. I should try to worry less. I am sure everything will work out for the best. Things have a way of sorting themselves out in the end. And Father is such a bright man. Bright, wealthy and lonely. Such a combination attracts scavengers.

And as if this has not been enough of a worrisome bother, we held our engagement party at the Rutherford's in the end of October. The party was lovely, in fact spectacular. But Mrs. Rutherford has a unique way of making me feel childish and wholly undeserving to be a part of their family. Please do not tell that I feel so. I tried once to talk to Artie about it, but he dismissed it as rubbish and said I need not bother myself; she just comes off that way. He is so adorable. He told me the only Rutherford I need worry about was already impressed. Of course, he meant himself. How I wish I had a shoulder somewhere to cry on. I think a few good, shared tears would help ease my mind. Times like this I miss Mother and you the most. Times are what times are, though. I guess our burdens are each our own to bear and since I am no longer a child, I must learn somehow to carry mine. I just wish I could do it with such grace as Mother did. Perhaps in time.

I had better let you rest now. I hope to hear from you when you are able. Give all my love and best wishes to the family and I pray your Christmas is lovely.

Love always,
Maggie

CHAPTER TWO: 1899

12 February, 1899

Dear Cousin Rachel,

I hope this letter finds you in better health and spirits. I was so excited to receive your last letter. Do not worry with it being short. Recovery takes a long time and I do not want you to relapse on my account. Even just a few words warmed my heart. It is good to hear the ranch is prospering well. That should make things better. Please do not worry that you may not be able to come to my wedding. I know that you want to be here and that is the most important part. I promise to make a trip there to see you as soon as I can. But remember, if illness falls away and you wake up one morning fresh and bright again, then you will have no excuse not to be here! You have not mentioned much about your sickness and Father tells me not to ask. He obviously knows more than he will tell, but I do wish you could confide in me. I fear it is something dreadful and you want to spare my feelings. But just know, the truth could never be more frightful than my imagination.

However, I did catch a glimpse of the old you when you spoke about Jonathan the way you did. Why I never knew he had the reputation as a scoundrel. Your letter sounded near loathsome of him. Actually, I had not thought of him in ages, but I guess a match there is impossible. Too bad. We could have been sisters. I still would like to know more about his dark side and why you detest him so. I mean really, "A no good, rich tramp with the face of an angel and the heart of Satan." Goodness! I am not much for gossip, but there must be something behind that you have not told me yet!

Artie and I were speaking in the parlor a few days ago. It seems so difficult to believe that our wedding is approaching so quickly. There is still so much to do! Then he tells me that he believes he would like for us to have children straight away. That caught me by surprise. Seems like most men would rather wait a while before starting a family. Do not misunderstand me. I cannot wait to have children. Oh their tiny little hands and precious faces. Just the thought of it thrills me. It almost makes me want to hurry the wedding up, though I think that would be impossible at this stage! There is still so much to do.

Father escorted us last week to look at estate homes and properties. Father says we are welcome to stay here if we wish to build a new home, but there is much available right now and I am not sure what we will decide. Artie actually asks my opinion in the matter and says he will buy whatever will make me happy. That is so adorable. But I fear I am more sensible about it than he is. You should see the lavish estates he has considered. But Father said it is important for a man with Artie's family and potential future to maintain certain appearances. I would be happy in a little cottage so long as Artie loved me.

As promised, I have taken your measurements to Lavelle's and your dress will be made in the event you make a full recovery and run a mad dash to get here just before the ceremony. Otherwise, I will send it to you and you will still be my true maid of honor, if only in sentiment.

There is little new news of Mrs. Connors. She still attempts to drive her talons deeper and deeper into Father, but as yet, he has proven to have quite a thick set of armor. I wish he would neatly shut things off with her. He must know what she is after and it is obvious he cannot love her. He still speaks of Mother all the time, which annoys Mrs. Connors. I hear little mention of the late Mr. Connors. She has sent her sons off to school for the term and does not seem to even miss them. I ask frequently if she has heard word from them and how they are but she always tells me the same, "I am sure they are fine or the school would have notified me." Heartwarming, you think? Although I know that Mother and Father were pressured to send me to a girl's school for the finest education, I am glad they chose otherwise. Father always employed the educators. Remember Governess Prionne? She may have been strict, but she was still a sweet lady under all that fluff. I cried and cried when she left. I do not believe you got on quite so well with her as I did, but then you had a bit more mischief in you, too. Oh my, then came that wretch of a woman, Madam Cort. You made sure she did not stay long. Uncle Theodore was so angry with you and Father acted it, but he always thought it a bit funny. I think Father was rather proud of your creativity, at least. I guess those days are long passed. In the blink of an eye, I will be married with children of my own to worry for. If nothing else, I want to make sure that they enjoy and relish their childhood. Now, standing on this side of it, it seems like such a fleeting thing. Look at me. Perhaps I have the jitters. It will pass. I love Artie and I know this is the right thing to do. I wish you were here to share it with me.

Give all my love to the family and I will write again soon. Happy New Year. Can you believe it? 1899! I hope to hear from you soon.

Love always,
Maggie

14 April, 1899

Dearest Rachel,

Oh Rachel, I am so angry with that hideous woman. She has tried in every way possible to ruin my wedding plans. Every single thing I talk to Father about, she attempts to undermine. Every single thing. We were sitting in the parlor discussing the music for the symphony, and that Andre had offered to compose our wedding song, when she spouts in again. Mrs. Connors sees no need in the symphony performing for my wedding or reception. Father attempted to explain to her the expectations for a wedding of this stature. That appeared to insult her even more and she then suggested that if the Rutherford's are so prestigious, then perhaps they should pay for these 'unnecessary' frills. But Father gained a smug look about him and he said, "It is not the Rutherford's prestige that concerns me, it is the Baine's." You know how Mrs. Connors came up, but I cannot believe she would be so ignorant to Father's importance here. Why, our family is as old as the Rutherford's. In fact, I believe all this has made me feel more secure with Artie's mother. After all, her lineage is no more noble than mine. I may not be so progressive as she, but I value the traditions of my family, of my mother and father. That is something to be proud of, is it not? I cannot believe I ever felt unworthy or below their standard and for no other reason than Mrs. Rutherford's snobbish behavior. She merely acted better than me and I believed it. Artie was right; I did not need to worry with such a trifle. I am embarrassed now that I ever felt so. However, I do fear such actions were a betrayal to all my father is, placing him in less worth. I vow to never be embarrassed or ashamed again, should I even meet Queen Victoria, herself!

I am sorry. Sometimes I do go on and on. Perhaps I am nervous about the wedding. I feel as if July 2 will be here in the wisp of a bird's wings and yet each day ticks slowly by, like the old clock in the parlor. Most everything has been planned now. Lavelle's is altering Mother's dress for me. It still looked so beautiful, though there were a few places where the old lace had frayed. My Grandmother wore the dress as well, Nanna told me. I did not know. Nanna was a young house girl back then. She plans to come with me to my new household. I will need her if we are to start a family right away. I couldn't imagine being without her. She is the nearest to a mother I have now, and you know she loved Mother very much. I have depended much on her with all this planning. She somehow can remember everything. I would certainly be lost without Nanna, and she has little to say about Mrs. Connors. In truth, I think Nanna will fancy putting some space between her and Mrs. Connors. I do not think she would like serving in Mrs. Connors household at all. She treats Nanna rather poorly, should you ask me, snapping her fingers and always complaining that her tea is too sweet. I think Nanna puts an extra dip of sugar in it just for spite now, but she'd never admit to it.

I cannot understand why Father trusts her so when she shows herself over and over. I think she cannot wait until I am married and moved out. It makes me want to persuade Artie to build a new Estate on that lovely property we noticed. It could take months or even more than a year to build enough of the home to be habitable. Now that could trim her claws a bit. Oh, I can imagine the look on her face, us saying that we'll be staying on until the master wing is completed. Then I could be right here to intrude on all her plans.

I know I mustn't think in such ways, but the temptation to return her malice overwhelms me sometimes. But look at me, going on and on about myself. I must know how you are feeling now. I wish I understood your ailment better. Could it be because you have moved so far from home? I have heard that people can become quite ill from homesickness. Your letter sounded so lonely, I wish I could visit. At least you do not have some woman attempting to ensnare your father. You have both your mother and father. That is something wonderful, is it not? I just know everything is going to be wonderful and beautiful for you. You must concentrate on your health for now, and then you will see.

That reminds me, I wish you would draw some pictures of those flowers you talk about. I cannot say I have ever seen anything like them, but the description sounds beautiful. I wonder how they seed. If you feel well enough sometime, perhaps you could watch and collect the seeds or bulbs and send some to me. If I could have some planted in our garden here, then I just know I would feel closer to you. I miss you so much. It is difficult to believe you have already been gone so long. I am certain that Artie will allow me to make a trip soon after we are married. He wants so much for me to be happy. I wish he could come as well, but I am sure he will have to stay. His work is so important; Father has put much trust in him.

I had better end. I cannot keep writing forever, but I wish I could. Once I stamp the seal, I am sure to think of a dozen other things I wanted to tell you and have forgotten. Please give my love to all the family.

Love always,
Maggie

3 June, 1899

Dearest Rachel,

I just received your letter and you sounded positively wonderful. I know you shall make a full recovery yet. I know I am selfish to still wish you could make the trip for my wedding, but it is more important for you not to relapse again. And yes, I find it rather funny that my present torment tickles you so. I guess it is true, no one's life is perfect, we all have our bothers. Maybe sometimes hearing about someone else's is refreshing. If it makes you feel better, I'll be sure to rant much more often!

In your letter, you said that Uncle Theodore will be gone for a few months, but you did not mention to where. I found myself curious. He surely has not gone off on some kind of Indian raid or anything, has he? We hear all sorts of rumors here. Sometimes the stories I hear in Lavelle's are enough to make me want my lamp lit all night. Nanna says it is all a tub of horse droppings, and I am sure she is right. In fact, I've never heard any such tales from you. But, true or not, I have every intention on visiting you after my wedding, once Artie and I are settled. I have spoken to him about it and he believes it is a wonderful idea, though he prefers it if Nanna will come with me, as he does not want me to make the journey to and from alone.

You should have heard Nanna make a fuss about that. "Lord, you don't know what you're talking about. What good's an old woman to chaperone like that? I 'spect I could hit someone with an iron pan, if it came to it." She is adorable; I just love her so much. She has no use for trains, though, thinks they go too fast. But you know Nanna, she is not comfortable on anything except her own two feet.

I am excited. We have decided on the old Barkley Estate. You should recall it. It is north of town, past the apple grove; the one with the stone fence and arch. Eloise Barkley past on last year and they lost their only son back in Gettysburg and he had never married. She has a cousin, but they already have a fine estate down in Maryland, so Artie just signed all the necessities last week. I tell you, I think that was the first test of patience and we haven't even exchange vows yet. He went on and on about all the details of owning and buying property. Poor Artie just doesn't understand, I find it difficult to decide what pattern I want for a new dress and even then I can spend hours and hours contemplating fabrics and buttons and lace. But the home is exquisite. When you are well enough to come, you will enjoy your own sweet in the south wing. Nanna's quarters are even beautiful, but she thinks them a bit much. Well, she says that, but I believe she will like it quite well. There is a lovely terrace stretching all around the sides and across the back, where every room on the second floor steps out to the fresh air.

Father was pleased with the choice and felt it will make a respectable home for engagements and such. Artie's mother gave her typical curt smile. She had her eye on another property much closer to them. But it was not nearly so grand or magnificent. All the same, I am nervous about leaving home. Father says the he and Mother attended many functions at the residence and Mother always thought it had a lovely charm, if properly decorated. Still, mother having been there is not the same as my memories of her playing in the garden with me, or us dancing across the floor, playing while Father worked. I will not be able to imagine her small figure or auburn ringlets falling gracefully, framing her face while she smiled in that loving manner she always had.

I sound spoiled. But I cannot help what is in my heart. With all the excitement and anticipation of becoming Artie's wife, of starting a family of our own, with each passing day I also feel this heaviness. Some days I am nearly overwhelmed, so much so, I just want to run to Father and cry. But do you think he would understand? When I leave, I'm afraid the presence of Mother our home still embraces may evaporate once that conniving harlot pushes her way in. She is sure to change everything, erasing every resemblance of my mother. I know it is terrible for me to despise her so, but I cannot help it. I see the greed in her eyes every time she walks through the parlor or perches herself in Mother's favorite chair, complaining that it is uncomfortable and poor quality. That chair was brought over from the old world and is worth half the estate Mr. Connors left behind, even before his debts were secured.

I cannot believe that in just one month I will be spending my first full day as Mrs. Arthur Rutherford. Artie does not seem bothered at all, always smiling and sweet mannered as ever. Then again, I do not know if it is so difficult for him to leave home. He already resides in a guest cottage, preferring privacy over grander comforts. I like that about him. I fear we shall have too much privacy in our new home. We could spend days wandering and never see one another. It is beautiful, but I do not know what we will do with so much. I know, our house is not exactly tiny, but it has never felt so open and vast. Perhaps when I'm allowed to work with some decorators, then we can make it feel more comfortable.

I think this is the worst part. Everything is done. Well, everything but the final set up. All the dresses are made, the suits are done, the catering ordered, even the music decided. I must feel strained because there is nothing left for me to do to occupy my mind. I know you understand what I mean. I don't want to feel frightened. I love Artie and there is no question in my heart that he is the only man I will ever love, but, well, I don't know what it is. Perhaps it is leaving my home and that attachment to my Mother. Do wish me luck. I am sending your gown and I want you to wear it on July 2nd, please. Knowing that you shall will make me feel you are here with me in spirit. I hope it fits well. I cannot wait to hear from you. Please give the family all my love and tell them I wish they could be here as well. I miss you all so much. Take care and continue with your healing, please.

Love always,
Maggie

5 August, 1899

Dearest Rachel,

Thank you so much for the beautiful blankets. I have never seen anything so unusual. The colors are remarkable and the images so native. These will be a certain treasure in our new home.

Oh there is so much to tell you, I can't imagine how I shall start. I am pleased that your dress arrived and you found it such a pleasant fit. I hope you make good use of it. Artie says I might come to see you in the spring. There is still so much to do here with settling in our new home and decorating. It seems there is a constant stream of people come to paint this or that, deliver furnishing, hang tapestries; I cannot keep up with all the bustle, but I try. Father says it is important that I maintain the proper dignity as the mistress of our home, giving approval and disapproval as it fits. He even said that sometimes it sets people right if you find their initial efforts unacceptable, that they will think twice at attempting to cheat you in the future or take advantage of your kindness. But I am finding this task difficult. I just loathe telling someone that I do not like what they have done. It all seems like so much work to me. Still, I have taken his advice and I fear a few of the help may perhaps be ready for a mutiny.

I see myself complaining. Rather childish, do you think? I know how lucky I am to be the mistress of this estate and Mrs. Arthur Rutherford. I still cannot believe it. I so wish you could have been here to share it with me. That is the only thing that could possibly have made the day more beautiful. Lavelle's did wonderful work restoring Mother's gown and it fit so well that I felt it was made for me. Yet, it was rather like having Mother and Grandmother here with me, also.

Father looked so handsome as we walked towards the alter. And Artie, well seeing him looking at me as we walked toward him, it made my heart flutter and my stomach tingle. I never even noticed all the guests surrounding us, and there were more than four hundred people attending. They somehow were lost in a distant fog that seemed to begin right about where the pews began. After all the time of planning and the lavish expenses, I noticed nothing apart from my father and Artie. Even the priest's voice sounded like an echo from a dream. When Artie took my hand, we left this world somehow.

Perhaps that is the binding of God, the moment where he joins our two souls for life. I felt as if we stood at the alter of heaven itself in the mist of the clouds with God and His host of angels peering into our very hearts. We stood, reciting our vows, amidst the honesty and purity of our love. Now I cannot wait for you to marry as well.

The grand reception following lasted well into the evening hours. I do not know what time we were finally off, but Artie had arranged a lovely white and gold carriage, charged by a team of twelve Arabians. The horses were all white with their manes plated and tasseled and the front of the team bore blankets with the Rutherford Crest on them. I felt like a queen riding away, with all the crowd cheering and waving, but my heart panged somewhat as I caught Father's eye. I knew we'd have brunch the next morning and then Artie and I would be off to the country for two weeks.

Artie has some important business still at the firm and could not spare the time for a trip abroad, but has promised we shall go next summer for our anniversary and spend a month in Europe.

Now, you must not show this letter to anyone else, at least not this page because I must tell how frightened I was about our wedding night. Well, now I know why Father kept attempting to bring up the subject but fell short of actually divulging anything. Of course, I knew things happened and husbands and wives were together in their own way, but I felt so foolish. I still do. It is not like the little kisses that seem to tickle from the inside out. Oh, it seems to make him happy enough, but I find it rather clumsy and confusing and well, I cannot think of any other way to say it but, messy. I know this is awful of me. I've just told you how beautiful and wonderful and spiritual our wedding was, but while the wedding day may be for the bride, the wedding night is obviously for the groom.

It is times like this I miss Mother most. I know she would have told me more what to expect and perhaps what was expected. I wish I did not feel quite so embarrassed. But Artie seems to enjoy watching me blush. I am blushing now! I am certain that I will work this out in time. He is sure to tire of the adventure and will not require such frequent episodes soon enough.

Now I have said so much to embarrass myself that I fear I cannot write any more. It is just that I really have no one here I feel close enough to with whom to discuss such things. I would never talk to Mrs. Connors about this. Oh my, the thought of her marrying my father after what I know now, I do not believe my sanity could withstand it. He is certain to see through her conniving methods soon.

She tried her best to interfere between Father and I during the wedding, even wanting to sit in the place that would have been Mother's. We had arranged to have a red rose lay across her seat in her memory. You should have seen the little tantrum she had, even though we had planned this from the beginning. She thought that we could just move the rose down one seat, instead. Of course I said no, but father did, too and they were not on good terms all evening. That was about as lovely a wedding present as she could give, though. Since Father was annoyed with her, he felt no guilt leaving her to her own devices while we danced and mingled with the guests. Father spent a great deal of time talking to Artie's family who had traveled here for the wedding, too.

But, it appears they have mended their tiff, as Mrs. Connors has once again resorted to her fallacious kindness. Certainly Father will put it all together before he finds himself trapped in her clutches. I cannot imagine them standing in a cloudy mist before God. I fear it is not heaven that woman would drag Father into.

Well, there is much to do. I am so happy to hear you are feeling better all the time. I do wish I could help you in some way. You help me so much every time I receive a letter. Why, when the post arrives and I see your script, it fills me with a girlish happiness, like when we played in the gardens, hiding from Nanna.

Please give my love and best wishes to your family and I am glad Uncle Theodore's trip was both safe and successful. Best wishes and I hope to see you in the Spring.

Love always,
Maggie

2 October, 1899

Dearest Rachel,

It is so wonderful to hear you restored and active again. I floated through the house all of yesterday, happy with your news. I must say, though I am surprised to learn of your suitor. I am sure he is quite pleasant, but it is Uncle Theodore that holds my concern. However, he has always been more progressive than Father in the matters of foreigners. You know how father distrusts most anyone here from abroad. Senior Miguel Ferdinando. I am not sure how to say it, but it looks lovely. The way you told of his accent, why it sent a chill across me. I promise I blushed though I were all alone in my sitting room. He sounds romantic and handsome. It is so good to hear you happy again. I have long awaited such a letter to come. Perhaps I want everyone as elated and in love as I am with Artie.

He is well, speaking of my dear husband. I never tire of saying that, it is still so fresh and exciting. However, he works too much and sometimes cannot come home until well after nightfall. I can recall Mother greeting Father at the door, even in late hours, with a smile and warm kindness; I try to do the same.

The estate is coming along well. I have seen over the completion of the family wing. I believe I shall take a week's rest from the noise and bustle before beginning anew with the guest wing. I hope it all will be completed before Christmas. I do so want our first Christmas to be perfect. This way we can coincide our Welcoming Party with delightful Christmas decorations and music.

Of course, Mrs. Connors turns her nose up when I mention plans for the event. I haven't any inclination as to why she is so bothered about my spending my husband's money. I had always thought her just selfish and wanting to horde father's money for when she could get her talons on it. But evidently, she really just dislikes me having things that I want. Perhaps she is jealous of her own upbringing or even upset at the money Artie draws from the firm. She does not understand that I do not truly care for the large estate and all the tending it requires of me to be its mistress. Nanna heads most of the servants, but I select all the furniture, rugs, papers, tapestries, linens and everything. I certainly wish the last residents had shown better taste and that their heirs may have left a little more furnishings behind. It would have made things much easier. The point is, I would be happy in a hole so long as I had Artie. Well, perhaps not an actual hole, but with much less, anyway. I only do all this for him. It is important because of our families and his future. Father thinks he may could be president some day. Though, if it is all the same, I'd rather he not. I get so tired when the men start on with their politics and such. Oh dear, if Artie were to stray into that profession, I fear I may never hear a conversation I truly understand again. But of course, I will support him no matter.

Now, in answer to your last question, no. I am not in the family persuasion as of yet. Though, it is not for a lack of effort from Artie. I had thought the new would wear off by now. I fear it is me. Perhaps I am doing something wrong, or perhaps it is more than that. I haven't told Artie this, but I'd rather not have a child just yet. I know I said I could not wait and the thought of a beautiful little darling is so wonderful, but I want to spend time with Artie for a while. I also wish to visit you in the spring and we have planned a beautiful trip to Europe for our anniversary. I believe afterwards would be a better time to start our family. I know that is selfish of me. Perhaps I am spoiled.

None the less, I could not travel in such a condition and afterwards I would need to wait until our child is old enough to travel or otherwise remain with Nanna. I am not sure I would wish to spend so long parted from a child, though. Mother did not leave me.

I wonder when all my happy moments will cease to be bittersweet. Somehow my thoughts always turn to her. When I look to know how to act or what to do, I try to recall what my mother did. Artie's mother has more than an ear's full of advice she barrages upon you as often as she casts her disapproving glare.

I know she thought with my mother passed on, she could influence me, pull me into her progressive cause. But I have no desire to begin pelting every man I meet with all her ideas of women voting and holding offices in government. It is not so much that I think she is wrong. I believe women can be quite cunning in their own right and should have their own vote to cast. I just do not wish to fight that battle myself and I do not care for the way she goes about it. Men are afraid of aggressive women and that is why we haven't been given the vote, if you ask me. It is not because they think we are foolish. It is because they fear we are smarter than they and may not be able to control how we use our vote. Mrs. Rutherford does not understand that. So, she harasses everyone she sees of importance, which are many, but it is in their eyes that they only tolerate her because of her husband and his money. Her husband even laughs about her sometimes. But she is serious, avidly so. Why, she even suggests that in a hundred years time, not only will women vote, but that they'll be president as well. Father laughed and laughed when Artie told him about that tirade she had last month. It was a bit embarrassing. We were there for an afternoon tea party when it all went a bit sour. I think she'd been into the tonic a bit, if I were to guess.

Oh look at me. Marriage is turning me into a gossip. There is a fine line between news and rumor, so I'd best watch myself before I create a scandal large enough to span the whole distance between us.

I cannot wait to hear more about Miguel. Now that you are feeling better, I shall expect longer and more frequent posts from you. Give my love to your family.

Love always,
Maggie

10 December, 1899

Dearest Rachel,

How exciting. I just received your letter and the news is glorious. I cannot wait to tell both Father and Artie tonight. I think it extraordinary for you to find a man so handsome and charming after moving off like you did. I was a bit afraid, especially from your letters early on, that Texas was completely devoid of eligible and worthy men to marry. Yet, I always knew in my heart that a lady as lovely as you would draw the attention appropriate to your house. I do not know much of Texas wealth nor about Mexico, but Miguel does appear to have a good station. That is always important, Father says. I know Uncle Theodore would never let you go about with a scoundrel, anyway.

Married. Such beautiful news. I only wished you had told me beforehand, then I perhaps could have made a racing trip to stand with you. I know you were unable to attend my wedding, but that illness was no fault of your own. However, it is likely for the best. I have a secret to tell. Not even Artie knows yet, though I will be sure to have told him by the time you receive this, so it will be safe to go ahead and spread the news.

We are in a family way. I am positive now. I had been waiting, just to make sure. I'd hate to give out that sort of news and be wrong! Nanna is sure of it and I expect I shall be bearing a tiny bundle of crying joy come sometime in June. Of course, this changes all my plans for the coming year. I cannot see Artie letting me travel in the spring. Oh, I would hope not. Can you imagine the scandal of presenting a baby on a train? Oh, no. That would not do at all. I shall have our little one right here. We've a nice little sitting room in or suite and I think it will make a lovely nursery.

I am most amazed at feeling no disappointment about having to postpone our trip abroad. Perhaps, if Miguel will allow it, you could come to visit me this spring and stay, since I'll not be fit for travel. That would be so wonderful. I would love to have you here with us. Just think of the lovely shopping and all we could do together. And now that we are both married, we could go to the Bistro for tea without being run out. Oh, I hope you can come.

In other events, I fear that my taking a new home has left my Father ever more at the mercy of that dreadful Mrs. Connors. I hear he sees her almost daily and she has been known to spend several days at a time in the guest quarters of our home. I know, I do not live there any longer, but it is still my home. It is my deepest concern that Father will marry the foul creature and bring her to ravage my dear mother's abode. I have had to spend so much time here, and rightly so as it is with my husband that I belong, yet perhaps if I could visit Father more frequently, then I could find a way to prevent this from happening. I just know there is a way to stop it. There must be.

It is beyond my ability to understand how it is that Father cannot see through this woman and understand what she is truly after. She cannot love father at all. In fact, I see her contemptuous looks every time we are all together. However, to be fair, it may be because of me that she looks so displeased. I fear it is no secret to her what my feelings are on the matter. But how could hey be anything else? After all, just consider all the vile things she said about me and her vicious attempts to ruin all my wedding plans. Do you think I am wrong to dislike her so?

My asking this of must mean that I am, questioning myself, however. Really, do you think I have been unfair to Mrs. Connors? I cannot recall ever liking her. Perhaps that was not the best way to start and I must accept the inevitable, she is likely to become my Father's new bride at any time.

I want Father to be happy, really I do. If this beast of a woman can do that, then I must swallow my own pride and selfishness and let it be. But I fear he does not see what she really is about. I truly do not wish to dislike her so.

Oh, this is confusing. I am so positive that she is after what my father has rather than him and he may discover such a travesty too late. His heart will be broken by it, but he does no listen to me when I try to speak to of it. I am sure he believes me merely jealous because I do not want her replacing Mother in his heart. But I know that cannot ever happen. No woman, despite beauty and charm could ever usurp my mother. They loved one another so much.

Perhaps I shall try to see the good points of Mrs. Connors. It will show Father that I am trying to get along with her. If nothing else, should my efforts fail to prove Mrs. Connors to be a well intentioned woman, then Father might look at reason rather than loneliness as a means to judge her character.

Oh, that is enough of that. I am so happy I have the opportunity to mull over these ideas with you. I almost hear your voice in my mind and what I know you are sure to answer with every question I write. You are the sister of my heart, this is certain.

Please let me know as soon as possible if you believe you may be able to come this spring or even summer. It would be so lovely. I do miss you so much and we've much to catch up on. I cannot possibly write all of everything in these letters, they would trail on and on into forever. Congratulations once again. I shall send you a wonderful gift. I cannot wait until tomorrow to go and search it out.

And I do plan on telling Artie this evening, after Father leaves, about our little guest that shall arrive soon. I know he will be so excited at the news. He so wanted to start a family right away. Perhaps you shall have the same surprise before you know it, as well.

I had better set off now. I must begin preparations for tonight. We plan to have our party on Christmas Eve. I wish you and your new husband could be here for it. I fear there is not enough time to make the arrangements for travel, however. But if you can, by any chance of fate, then know that you are welcome. Give my love to the family and to your new husband. I hope to hear from you soon.

Love Always,
Maggie

CHAPTER THREE: 1900

Dearest Rachel,

I cannot believe you are moving to Mexico. How on earth shall I write to you there? Does the post carry so far? I hope so. I do not wish to sound spoiled or anything, but I had so hoped you could make it here this spring. I understand, though. Once married, the husband's life seems to overtake your own. I feel that way often. I always thought marriage would provide some sort of freedom. I dreamed of being able to go and do as I pleased, but it is not hat way at all. So I understand, but you must endure a certain amount of pouting on my part.

Father is beside himself at becoming a Grandfather. He never ceases buying things for our coming arrival, much to the displeasure of Mrs. Connors. I hate to tell that they have announced a short engagement and are to be married in May. I have tried to be good and come along well with Mrs. Connors, but it is frightfully difficult. What is worse is that I think my endeavors have only helped her sink those sharp and ugly laws further into Father. Perhaps he now believes that I approve of the letch.

There is nothing more to do now, though. I have

resolved myself to the fate, but I just cannot make myself call her anything aside from Mrs. Connors. What will I do when she is married to Father? I do not believe it will be most appropriate to continue calling her Mrs. Connors and I cannot bring myself to say Mrs. Baine. That is absolutely horrible.

Enough of my trifles, however. I am pleased you enjoyed the gift that we sent, and Father, too. I am most pleased that they arrived unbroken. I have no idea how easy it is to obtain fine crystal and china out there, but wanted to make sure you had the best setting. Now you can host the finest table in Mexico! Our table is set with a similar pattern by the same maker, imported from the Far East. The crystal stemware is lovely, also. That design was not available when I picked out mine or I would have it as well. As it is, I bought every piece available to send to you, so if I want any for myself, I must wait for a new order to arrive.

I cannot wait to hear more about Mexico. I found it a tantalizing adventure when you moved to Texas, but now a new country as well. Miguel sounds quite important, but with such poor English, how, under heaven, can you communicate so well? Have you been able to learn his language? My, what language does he speak? In France they speak French, in Italy, Italian. I cannot but wonder because I have never heard of Mexican as a language. I shall ask Artie this evening. I am positive he will know. Sometimes I despise being an ignorant woman. Though I do not say it, sometimes I find myself more and more compelled by Artie's mother's ideals about women. It does seem foolish that so much remains hidden away from us merely because we are feminine. Artie does talk politics to me, but I have found over the months that his attitude of our discussions has slowly changed and I feel more like a child than ever. I think he is humoring me, perhaps he always did and I was just too naive to realize it.

The physician has me cooped up in he house now,

fearing I might birth early. He wants me here and the midwife is staying in a suite in the guest wing. I'm not sure that he was not put up to it, though. A month ago, Artie made a terrible comment to me, it hurt my feelings so deeply. I wanted to go out together for a stroll in the evening air, for it felt quite mild out to be January. But he said he thought it a poor idea and that I wouldn't want to parade about in my condition, that it would not do for people to see me such.

Why would he say a thing like that? Being with child is not shameful, well, not if you are properly married, of course. And come to recall, he said something about the party we held at Christmas as well. I had just begun to reveal my nature and wanted a family dress to wear to the party, but he insisted that I wear a customary evening gown, merely fitted to conceal my weight. I did not think much of it at the time, but it comes together oddly, do you not agree?

Artie's mother is thrilled about my little, hidden surprise. Almost as excited as Father. The only times I have been out of the house is when she has come to fetch me. She has a way of overriding Artie that I do not. After all, it would be impolite to refuse his mother my company when she has requested it. I have decided that as bizarre as his mother might be, I enjoy her company more and more. That could be from the lack of other company I have to spend time with, too. I love Nanna, but she is busy overseeing the house and all the servants. The renovations are long since completed and now I sit most of the days alone, surrounded by fine tapestries and furniture that do not say or do anything. They merely sit there, as happy to be admired as not and I'm slowly feeling more in common with them than anything else.

I do sometimes hear the servants singing in other halls while completing chores, dusting and polishing. But if Miss Grafiender, the midwife, gets wind of it, she quickly hushes it up, chiding the staff and saying I need quiet and rest.

I cannot wait to have this baby. Then there will be noise and happiness in these halls that only echo silence. Perhaps the joyful sounds of a child will cheer my heart. I look forward to it more and more with each passing day. Nanna thinks we shall have a boy. I hope we do. We shall name him Arthur Baine Rutherford, if so. We have not decided yet on a name for a baby girl. But whatever God brings us, I shall be happy.

I had best end here. Please be careful on your journey and write soon to tell me all about Mexico and the wonders there. You are so lucky in life, to have such opportunities to experience these wonderful adventures. I want to hear all about it. Give my love to everyone.

Love always,
Maggie

1 April, 1900

Dearest Rachel,

Oh, I am so furious. Not about your letter, of course. I perfectly understand the many obligations of setting a house in order and how difficult it can be. It is difficult enough when I know the servants understand me, but it must be an absolute nightmare attempting to communicate down there. I shall count myself lucky for enduring no more than I had to. I could just as well have been in your shoes. But you fit them much better than I. It is good to know they speak Spanish, however. When I asked Artie, he thought I was telling a joke and laughed at me. I felt far too embarrassed to admit my question was real. So thank you for the news.

But back to my fury. I knew it was coming, we have been debating it for so long and it has finally happened. Father married the trollop. Yes, she is now his wife and already trying to shuffle Mother's beautiful things out of the house. Of course, I wanted them if they just had to go and Father said yes, but she threw the biggest tantrum over it that I have ever seen. Can you believe she wanted to sell Mother's things in an estate auction? Many of the items have been in our family for generations, even back from the old world. I guess that is why she wanted to sell them, she thought she could pocket some extra money for her purse from it.

Well, I put my foot down there. Those are not her things. I shall not have that wretched woman selling my mother's favorite knitting chair or the dining furnishings that belonged to my great grandmother. I do not know where she comes up with this audacity. I hope Father makes it very clear in his will that she is to receive nothing from our estate, she can keep her inheritance from the late Mr. Connors and that should do her well enough, especially with the boys getting older now.

Artie tells me not to worry. He has been quite kind about it, even saying that if they did, by chance, slip into auction, he would make sure they came here. I think she believed that because I am so enormous with child at the moment and completely restricted to the confines of home, I would not find out until it was too late. You do not think that Father would have allowed her to do such a terrible thing, do you? I do not like to even contemplate that possibility.

I know. I must somehow manage to master this hostility. She is his wife now and if I want to maintain my wonderful relationship with Father, then it is not good to constantly make him feel torn. I have tried. I told you I would. But then again I placed far too much hope in father discovering by his own wits exactly how lecherous she is. She is only after his money. She wants Father to put her sons through their education and then die at an early age of the heart illness, not before she bears him another child, however. I know she thinks that is the key to winning his fortune.

Yes, yes, I can already hear you. I know I do not need Father's money. I have no idea what to even do with it. Actually, I wouldn't mind building a new hospital with better conditions, should the money fall into my lap. But I just do not want her to have it.

I promise, I did try. Every Sunday evening Father and Mrs. Connors came over for tea. Well, she was Mrs. Connors then; I feel uncertain what I should call her now. Perhaps Mrs. Baine will suffice for the time being. I paid her compliments on her dresses even though I found them rather dated. She would not even accept the compliments. All she managed was a little pursing of her lips and nodded back at me as though I had said something on the verge of indecent. Truth is, though they were dated, they did somehow suit her well and likely much better than these most flamboyant evening dresses or the uniform looking walking dresses. They were soft and slightly ruffled with a high collar made from embroidered lace. In fact, I had not noticed the dress before in such detail, though I am positive I have seen her wearing it at least once previous. The work on the lace is quite remarkable with beautiful detail. I would love to know where to find it because I have never seen anything like it at Lavelle's. But she simply refused to engage in any conversation with me.

I do not believe Father noticed a thing, but Artie did. He said he was quite proud of me for trying so to make Mrs. Connors comfortable in our home. Truth told, though, I do not believe that she is comfortable anywhere, at least not among the higher class. Nanna says that breeding outs itself and that someone can only masquerade for so long before the mask starts chipping away.

Oh, I just love Nanna. She is the wisest woman I know. It is funny to hear her talk about breeding and classes when she has lived her entire life as a servant, just like her mother before her. I do not know if she has any other family. You know her Papa died breaking a horse when she was small. He worked for Grandfather. But she never takes a leave to visit her family or anything. I've really always thought of her as our family. Artie is quite good about this as well. He knows how much Nanna means to me and even allows her a seat at our dining table so long as guests are not present. I really do not care about the guests, but Nanna says he is right. She still eats in the kitchen with the other staff more often or not. But I know it makes her feel good to be invited.

Well, here I am, chattering on and on again. I am writing in stretches for I tire so easily. You would not believe how huge I am right now, and the little creature inside there just will not stay still. He thrashes constantly, especially when I try to sleep. It must be a boy. I cannot imagine a little girl causing so much trouble!

Well, your new home sounds lovely. I think a beautiful ranch is just right for you, so long as you have access to shopping. I would really love to see you. Hopefully soon we will be able to figure out a way. Perhaps we can meet in the middle somewhere and spend a short time together. It is terrible to spend so long away from family. And speaking of family, give them my love as soon as you see or write to them. Please take care of yourself and good luck learning Spanish. Now that could have been a useful language. I am still perplexed at the necessity to teach us Latin! Tell Miguel hello for me.

Love always,
Maggie

29 May, 1900

Dearest Rachel,

Oh Rachel, I hardly have the energy to write, but I felt I must let you know at once. Yesterday we had our beautiful baby. Nanna was right, we have a wonderful and perfect son. We named him Arthur Baine Rutherford. I just cannot believe how perfect he is. He has a little sheen of blonde hair on his head. I never knew how much I loved him, even while he was still growing inside me. I cannot stand for him to be more than an inch away from my side, but the Midwife keeps trying to take and lay him in his bassinet in the sitting room.

Twice I have already been scolded for venturing in there and retrieving him. I just told them that if they would stop insisting on taking him away, then I would stop insisting on bringing him back to bed with me.

Everyone does seem to get up in arms every time I move, though. Little Arthur was a rather large baby and I know there were a few complications, but I do not believe anything serious.

Rachel, I just want to keep staring at him all the time. I feel him in my heart as though he were always there. Even though he has just arrived, I already find myself perplexed. I cannot recall my marriage with Artie without these little fingers and toes. Is that silly?

I just cannot wait for you to have this feeling, too. This is the grandest thing in the world. Don't be scared of the pain. The pain comes and then it is gone, but little Artie here, he stays. You need one, too. Now I know why Artie wanted to start a family as soon as possible.

Father is beside himself and he took Artie out to celebrate last night. Little Artie was born at four o'clock in the afternoon and he weighs about eight and a half pounds. Nanna says Father and Artie kept pacing up and down the hall space outside my door, frequently bumping into one another. I am sure it was a funny sight to see. Nanna said they were asking if it was over every five minutes, would not give anyone a moment's peace to get things done. I guess they were not so aware of how long the process can sometimes take. I really feel quite lucky. It only took about six hours. Nanna says that Mother pained for almost twenty hours when she had me. Now I know why I am an only child!

Oh, you should hear his little cry. It is precious, though

I can't stand him to want for anything. But I think he may be hungry. We will have to take care of that.

I just wanted to drop a note with our joyous news. Thank you for your prayers and letters. I must say, yesterday, all my prayers were answered, at least to date. Tell Miguel hello from the three of us and I do hope to see you as soon as possible. Please take care and send my love to the rest of the family.

Love always,
Maggie

25 July, 1900

Dearest Cousin Rachel,

Please forgive my not writing sooner. I fear I have been a bit frail since having little Artie. But please do not worry. It is only weariness. I tire easily and must rest often, but Dr. Carroll is certain I shall make a full recovery and chastises my notion that I should be able to run about so soon. The doctor has assured Artie that this is nothing unexpected or unusual and I shall soon enough be right again, in plenty of time to chase our little one through the halls.

I must say, I did not understand such a need for recovery. Why, I know that women out on farms and even slave women some years ago, would birth children and continue on working. Of course, Nanna tells me those things. She thinks it is because I have been so sheltered and pampered my whole life that my body has no idea what to do with real exhaustion. No, she does not mean it in a bad way. She is as guilty as any for keeping me sheltered. She just believes my body did not have the adequate preparation for such an event and I am recovering from one nasty shock! That is Nanna, is it not? I love her so much. She is wonderful help and so good with little Artie. I wish she had had children of her own.

She would have made a superb mother. But she insists that she made a choice not to marry and carry on with children.

We were talking in the sitting room just last week about it. I was resting on the chaise while she rocked little Artie. I know it is not my place to pry into other's lives, but Nanna is more family than servant, and she is the only person I can talk to here. It made me a bit uncomfortable, though, her answer did. She told me a sad story of how her family had come up from slaves and how her mother found work with my family when she was but a child, still. Then, of course, she married and they lived in the servant's quarters and raised Nanna there. Then as she grew, her mother taught her to work in the house as well and when her parents had passed on, she stayed here with us, seeing as it is all she has ever known. But she did not want to have children she could not afford to raise properly nor would she ever want them to serve a master.

I must say, I felt most awkward. I never thought of Nanna as serving us, at least not like that. But it is strange, is it not? How the person who seems closest to a mother to me is only here because she is compensated. Perhaps I am feeling overwhelmed with emotions, but it swelled inside and hurt me. At the same time, I cannot help but understand. Looking at little Artie, I would never want anything but the absolute best for him. She cannot be any different. I do not think any mother could be. I would not want to raise my son to be a servant, either. So that is one thing I have to be thankful for. Though I know my life has held many blessings.

It must be this insistent weariness that depresses me. I know I have led a privileged life and have no right to cry over the few burdens I've born. There are few things I cannot tolerate, but self pity is one of them. Yet, here I find myself weeping at the silliest happenings, little words or comments that I take to heart. Everything makes me feel so useless. And taking care of little Artie, well, Nanna has taken over so much of that, I feel left out sometimes.

But, then he cries and I do not know what to do, no one will show me or help me do it myself. They believe it is easier to just get it done and I'm sent off to my bed once more to rest.

Perhaps if I did not rest so often, I would not require so much! I just have this terrible fear that once little Artie is running and playing, it will not be me he runs to when he falls and hurts himself. Is that selfish? I know it must be. I just want to be his mother and I feel like everyone is taking it away from me.

And for goodness sake, I am crying already. I am sure to run out of tears soon. I do not know what is wrong with me. I do not feel anything physical, except the fatigue. The doctor thinks I am normal, just a little slower than some, but that he sees it frequently.

I look at little Artie and he fills me with so much joy. I tingle from head to toe. It is as though my life never truly began until he was placed into my arms. But then as quick as I hold him, someone is always coming to usher him away, preaching rest as they rush through the echoing hall. And echo it does. Despite the tapestries, rugs, paintings and such, I always hear the footfalls continue to trickle, long past the presence of the steps. I think it may be a trick of my mind or of my heart. I ache inside when little Artie is not near. Foolish sounding, I know. There are so many who would love to have the help I have and the love of my family. Artie worries over me when he comes home. But he does seem to come in later and later.

Nanna simply will not allow me to meet him at the door, as I like to do. In fact, I am quite lucky to sit in the garden for a while if the weather is fair. And that is only because the doctor insisted to Nanna that the fresh air is good for me.

Yes, it is funny how you think marriage will bring freedom, yet I have never felt more imprisoned. It is not that I am unhappy, exactly. Please do not think that. I love my husband, I love my precious son, I love Nanna and have even become quite fond of our additional staff. I just want to enjoy it all, too. What is the point of being surrounded by such wonderful beauties if you are never allowed to enjoy them? It is torturous.

Oh, my dearest Rachel, this must sound so dreadful. I apologize. I am happy, just perhaps a little tired. I am quite sure things will look better tomorrow. Mother always said, "The beauty of going to bed at night is leaving all the troubles from the day behind. The morning sunshine will make everything new again." So perhaps tomorrow will be new and me along with it.

I shall write again soon. I fear my energy is spent. Give my love to your family and your lovely husband, Manuel. I do so look forward to meeting him soon.

Love always,
Maggie

20 September, 1900

Dearest Cousin Rachel,

Oh, it is so wonderful to hear from you. The villa sounds absolutely marvelous. You describe it with such vision, I can almost smell the trees. I do so hope to see it one day. You need to draw a picture of it for me. I do not believe there is anything with that architecture here I can compare it to. You sketch so well, I am positive you can do it justice, so do not even complain or attempt to deny my request.

Little Artie is growing quickly. I cannot believe how rapidly it passes. But still, my health is much better, so I have taken charge over him. I think all I really needed was to get my blood fired up a bit. These ladies in our keep are ever too ready to take him off my hands and I feared I would miss all the beautiful moments that are meant for a mother to enjoy. Well, I could not have that. So I simply started running them out of my room. You would not believe how they would flock every time Little Artie gave so much as a whimper. Always, "You need your rest, Madam," or some such rubbish. I think I felt melancholy for my baby. Once I began shunning off those little bees, I felt the fatigue drip away. Before I knew it, I felt as though drapes had been opened and the bright sun shone in. Rest! 'Twas not rest I needed at all. Plain and simple pining for my child, and that is it. And it does no more good to see others taking on the duties that ought to be mine, either. Mind you, when you have your own, do not let any nurse maid run you out of your child's nursery. It will cause an illness no medicine can cure.

But Little Artie, he certainly knew what I needed. Wrapping my arms around him is like breathing life itself. I do not know how to explain it. I cannot imagine life without him, as if life never existed before he came to us. Every little noise he makes, I know it. I feel so complete holding him, warm all the way through my body and into my soul. It is amazing how I never knew he was missing before. I do not know how my heart managed to beat or my soul exist when I knew him not, for I feel he has always been part of me. My little, dearest one. You will understand soon enough, I suspect.

Now that I am better, we are planning Little Artie's christening soon. It shall be a wonderful event with a truly grand celebration to present our little heir. Artie is so proud of him, though I believe he hardly knows what to do with one so small. He looks terribly awkward attempting to hold his son, but I am sure it will all right itself soon enough as little Artie grows and becomes more sociable.

I do miss you, Rachel. Of course I have other friends and cousins, but no one takes your place. I just cannot find myself discussing all these matters with them. When it comes to it, I have to consider the adversity of gossip and there is no one else that I can trust with such intimate details of my life. I do not want all of Lavelle's discussing every little concern I have. There is Artie to think about and his career. Such gossip simply will not do, though I dare say enough goes on without any help at all.

In fact, I heard from Cousin Marlene just last week that rumor had gone saying I was deathly ill and would not live long. This seemed to be incredible news, as that meant the charming Mr. Arthur Rutherford II would be a widower and soon in need of a new wife. Can you believe that? Those giggling little shagnasties! I know, I shouldn't say such a thing, but still. They were thrilled at the prospect of my death just to get their greedy little claws into my husband. So you see, I must watch with great concern who I confide in. I fear I do not trust anyone aside from you, Nanna and Artie. But I guess it is best to keep the things close to your heart in good trust. I cannot even talk to father any longer, for I fear his precious bride has more than a small hand in my declining popularity.

Artie's mother tells me not to worry over it, that our family is both wealthy and powerful, which makes a delicious combination for the serpent tongue of the jealous. In this, I believe she may prove right. I do not treat people any differently than I ever have, but I find that I am treated in a new fashion, one that does not settle so well with me, either.

But as Artie's wife, I have no right to complain. It seems rather silly to do so. There are those who are unfortunate, with little food or without shelter and proper clothing. Yet I sit away pining over the lost freedom of girlhood and those afternoons giggling with you in the garden.

I am spoiled to the bone, that is it. Do you suggest anything to cure it? I wish Mother were here. If for nothing else, to be rid of that nasty step mother. I know, I know. I promised to try and I am, but she has been no help whatsoever. I believe we will eventually settle into a mutual, quiet disdain for one another and leave it at that. All I want is for Father to be happy and he does seem happier with her than he did alone. That is all that truly matters, is it not? Now if I could only convince my heart then the matter would be settled.

Oh my. I had best leave off here. Little Artie is awake, I hear him stirring. Please take care and write soon. I so look forward to your letters. They warm my heart for days on end after they arrive. Give my best wishes and love to your family and your new husband.

Love always,
Maggie

15 November, 1900

Dearest Rachel,

I am so excited! I just received the post and the letter telling of your arrival. I cannot wait to see you. It is long since time for a visit. I wish you would stay longer. I hope you find time to spend a few nights with us. Two weeks is a quick stay for such a long journey, but I know your husband is busy. Oh, it is only five weeks until you are here. I cannot wait to tell Artie when he comes home. What a wonderful surprise. We must plan a Christmas brunch for the family.

I do hope the weather cooperates with your travel plans. We have already had considerable snow this year, but I doubt that stops the locomotives. I still do not envy you that accommodation. They travel so fast and with such a loud, roaring sound. I can't imagine what it must be like to eat and sleep on that a contraption. Though, hopefully when little Artie is older, I will make the trip to visit you. Of course, I'd bring my little darling with me. It would be worth daring the frightful locomotive just to see your new home and spend time alone with you.

Be prepared when you arrive. Father is not looking well at all. I am not so sure his new bride is taking adequate care of him. Every time I see him, he looks pale and gaunt.

I fear he has an illness but he refuses to discuss it. Even Artie attempted to persuade him to visit a doctor, but he just will not. It breaks my heart. I can see the melancholy in his eyes. The only time he looks at all like his old self is when he holds little Artie, but still his strength seems to fail quickly. I do not know what to do. I am sure you will see what I speak of.

Oh, Rachel, I cannot abide the thought of losing my father. And then there is that wretched woman to contend with. She insists that he is fine and, "looks healthy as a horse to me." Can you believe that? Nanna calls her a black widow. I do not think so grand of her, myself. I prefer the term leech. Perhaps you or Uncle Theodore will able to persuade father that a visit to the doctor would not hurt. Maybe that will be just the thing Father needs, all the family here for Christmas.

Artie and I plan to have a grand reception for New Years. I think it is perfect that you will be here for it. We hope to make it an annual event. Most of the preparations will already be done before you arrive, but I'd love you to help with the last minute details. We will definitely have beautiful gowns sewn at Lavelle's. I'll have mine done early, though. I am afraid if we both came in so late, she would not have time to finish. But I will let her know that you will be in right after you arrive.

This is the most wonderful gift I could ask for. I am positive it will lift Father's spirits and mine are already soaring. Why, I'll be singing until your departure, I am sure. I cannot wait to see little Tildie, too. I have heard she has grown into a little lady. That is difficult to believe considering the sprout she was when you left. Time has passed quickly. Funny how we spent so much time pretending to be all grown up, with tea parties and our fancy little brunches together. Now we are grown and all I want to do is play like when we were children. Not that I would ever wish to give up the blessings I have in my life, but I would not mind a few more moments of the giggling innocence we held in our youth.

I will begin preparations right away. As I said, you simply must stay with us for at least a few days. I would prefer you made residence here in our guest wing for your whole trip. I know that Father has plenty of room and you would like to be there with your parents and family, though. So I promise not to have my feelings hurt. But you are most welcome here.

I had best end. It is little Artie's feeding time and he gets fussy if I am late. Be careful on your trip and I cannot wait to see you. Godspeed.

Love always,
Maggie

CHAPTER FOUR: 1901

20 January, 1901

Dearest Cousin Rachel

I do hope this letter finds you well. I wait eagerly for news of your safe arrival home, but could not wait another moment to write. Oh Rachel, Father has fallen gravely ill since your departure. He looked better than I had seen him in a long time while the family was here, but four days ago, he found himself too weak to rise from his bed. Word reached me late in the afternoon. Artie sent a messenger to the house and I went straight away.

Oh, my dear Rachel, you will not believe what I found when I arrived. That wretched woman. I swear I shall flail her myself. Had she sent for the physician? No. When I stepped into the house, I could hear her shouting at the staff, wanting to know when Father's attorney would arrive. The beast wanted to make sure that Father's will had been set to name her as the benefactor of our family estate. Can you believe her? I sent an errand boy straight away to fetch Artie. Well, I first sent for Dr. Carroll.

Oh, you should have seen the eruption she had when Mr. Baker arrived and then refused to discuss the contents of Father's will with her. Why, she shouted and called Mr.

Baker a number of things a lady ought not to say.

Dr. Carroll arrived and appeared quite displeased that she had left him in such a state without sending for help at once. And when she kept on with her shouting, Dr. Carroll told her he would have her removed if she could not master herself. Afterwards, we could hear her muttering horrible things while she stamped about the house. I attempted to pay no attention to her behavior and just see to Father's welfare until she turned her snake fangs on me. Can you believe she told me that I had no business there and that I should return home and leave Father to her, that she would see to him? Oh, I just could not restrain myself. Immediately I righted her. Why she did not even bother with sending for a doctor and she felt I should leave and let her tend to Father. And then, oh Rachel, I almost cannot bear to repeat what she said to me. I just cannot understand how he ever married such a wretched woman. She told me that calling for a doctor in his state was nothing but another waste of Father's money. Father's money, really. She believes it is her money and she is already counting it. There are so many things I would like to say about her, but I just cannot bring myself to write that sort of language. Though I am positive she would have no problem ranting out streams of obscenities if given the opportunity.

But I am a Bane and a Rutherford and I shall not sink to her low and disgusting level. But, if she believes she is getting her hands on my family's home, she is much mistaken. I am sure Father left her a tidy little sum to be getting on with, but he'll have not been duped. Artie, while he cannot say anything exactly, does work in Father's firm and has assured me that Father has taken care of everything properly. I just cannot handle that terrible woman destroying my mother's things.

Of course, the most important thing is that Father is a little better. He is resting. But I fear he shall not make a recovery. Dr. Carroll did not leave much room for hope.

My heart hurts so much. When Father is gone, I'll have no more parents. I know I have Artie and little Artie, too, but somehow I feel so alone. Artie may love me, but no one loves you like your parents. Father's arms have always been the safest place in the world. Yet, now I feel a terror that his arms cannot abate. I feel a loneliness creeping inside me that even his jovial laughter cannot push away.

This is selfish talk. I want Father to live for me, but I have grown and left him for a family of my own and what has he left? I feel guilty. I should have spent more time with him over this past year. Now it seems there is so little time left and I must battle for each second of it. I not only have his horrible nuptial mishap to deal with, but little Artie needs me, too.

I think I may have Nanna come and prepare my old room for me and the west room for little Artie. I would like him near me. Nanna can stay there as well. Who knows better how to care for Father than she?

Talking to you always helps to calm my spirit. I only wish you could be here to hold my hand through this. Perhaps I worry over nothing and Father will recover. That is a lovely thought. I had best leave off here. I know I could write into the deep hours of the night, I feel I shall not sleep. I will not require you to suffer the tedious chore of reading any further my ranting and crying.

I pray you have reached home safely and are well rested. Please send all my love to the family. I will send word of any changes here.

Love always,
Maggie

16 February, 1901

My Dearest Cousin Rachel and Family,

What I have feared for so long has finally happened. Father has passed from this world into heaven. It happened just last night. I feel the grief is so close, it chokes the air from my lungs. What shall I do without my Father? And little Artie, he will never recall the wonderful, playful grandfather I had so often prayed he would know and love.

I apologize that this letter is so brief, but I must write many more people and there are so many things that must be done. I cannot expect much help from his grieving widow.

I will write again soon, there is much to tell you.

All my love,
Maggie

17 March, 1901

Dearest Cousin Rachel,

I have meant to write several times since my last correspondence. I sit alone, with the best of intentions, yet nothing seems to appear on the parchment. The world just feels so different now and only Little Artie's laughter seems to pull me away from my melancholy.

Mr. Baker read Father's will last week. Father left his little bride a small stipend, but not the family home or estate. Turns out Father had purchased her previous home for her to live in once he had passed on. You know, she had to sell it in order to pay some of her previous husband's debts. Seems he had more debts in the closet than money in the bank. But Father left her cared for, at least until she remarries. I am positive that shall not be long in coming. After all, I cannot see her happy with enough for prudent living. But she made no objections or complaints. I guess she knew what to expect. I thought she would make an enormous fuss and rant and rave over every detail. I fully expected her to turn her hateful disposition on me.

A strange thing, though. While I expected the leach to

be angry and cold towards me, it is not her that appears the most affected. Artie has barely spoken to me since Mr. Baker discussed Father's estate. I am not really sure what troubles him. But you would think that I have enough to deal with, losing my father and all, without his distant behavior and cold remarks. I cannot imagine what it is that I have done to him. It makes me feel so alone.

Little Artie is playing on the floor by the hearth here in our room. You cannot imagine how he has grown. I wish Father could have held on to see this. I know it is wrong, but I feel so angry. Why could Father not believe that we were worth staying here to love and protect? Rachel, he gave up. He chose not to live any longer. Dr. Carroll said so. Father could have recovered if he had wanted to. What's worse, and please do not repeat this to a soul, but Dr. Carroll thought that Father perhaps had helped his condition along a bit. He did not want to live. I am just so angry and hurt inside. Why would he leave me? I wish I would have spent more time over the past year with him. Then perhaps he would have realized how much I need him.

But he did not stay and I must resign myself to this dreadful end. Little Artie needs me, but I fear my heart shall never be whole again. Part of it went forever away with Father.

I must meet again with Mr. Baker next week. It appears I must make some decisions regarding my inheritance. I wish Artie would attend with me, but he said he would rather not. Seems foolish to me. How am I to know what to do with properties and money? He refuses to discuss any part of it with me. If he were not a Rutherford, I would swear he was envious. Of course, I have heard his sly comments regarding his own father. I think Artie will be more than happy to take over his inheritance. I would rather give all the money away and have my Father home.

I am going on and on. I do not wish to depress you with all my problems. I am sure everything will seem better with time. Father always held such a strong face after Mother passed away. He still smiled at me and encouraged me to live, saying that Mother would never have wanted me to hide away in tears. It is so difficult to now be the one who must be strong. That is the circle of life, I suppose. Now it is my turn to be strong for my dear little one.

Life certainly does not take the turns we expected in our youth. We were going to get married and live next to one another, have a dozen beautiful children and wonderful parlor games on Saturdays. But I should not complain. Life is not all so horrible, and I may still have more children. Thinking about children, when do you plan to start your family? Oh, it is so wonderful. You will make such a marvelous mother. I cannot wait.

That would certainly bring some happiness to our tired family. I pray it is soon. How is everything with your husband? He is quite handsome and his accent is lovely. I enjoyed spending time with you over the holidays, though it was too short.

It is late. I have been waiting, hoping Artie would come home before I retired, but I fear he will be late again. I know his work is important. I had best leave off here. Please give my love to all.

Love,
Maggie

12 May, 1901

Dearest Cousin Rachel,

Thank you so much for your loving letter. I received it in this week's post. I am pleased to hear you are hoping for a baby soon. That is wonderful news. I will keep your wish in my prayers.

I shall soon have my first ride on a locomotive. Artie is taking us to the Pan Am Exposition in Buffalo. He has been invited as an honored guest and we shall tour the grounds with Mr. Roosevelt. I have never met the Vice President before, but Artie has. I wonder if his wife will attend as well. I am quite excited, though a bit nervous. I have heard so many rumors and reports. I have read in the newspaper that all the lights are just breathtaking and that it is supposed to be better than last year's exposition in Paris. I wish I could have gone to that one. I am sure it was wonderful.

Little Artie is going with us, but we are taking Nanna to watch after him. I do not wish to take him near so many strangers. There has been tell of a measles outbreak. Though I am sure we will not be near any of that.

I have also been invited to the Ladies Auxiliary Luncheon while we are there. I shan't know anyone. I fear it will be quite awkward but there is no way for me to decline. Artie shall be working. I am not exactly sure what he is doing, though. He mentioned that he will be meeting some important people and that is good for his career. So, if it is regarding his career, I consider it work. That is what he does most the time, anyway.

Artie has a new assistant at his office and they spend a terrible amount of time working. If it were a woman I would be quite jealous. As it is, my imagination gets the better of me sometimes and I fear he is out fraternizing with harlots. In my heart I know that is not true. But I wish he had a bit more time for Little Artie and me.

I wonder if Bill, that is Artie's assistant, is going to the Exposition as well. I know it is awful to say, but I hope he does not. Artie and I have spent very little time together since Father's death. I still miss him so much. It is difficult for me to believe he is really gone. Yet, I am trying to be strong for my family and not waste away in despair. Both of my Arties deserve better than that. And I know Father would never want me to pine so.

But, all the same, I still would prefer a little time alone with my husband. Things have not been better over the last couple of months. He is still distant and cold towards me. I tried to ask him why, but he just stared at me and then turned and walked out the door. I cried all through the night. I cannot imagine what it is that I have done to hurt him so. Please tell no one, but he does not even share a room with me any longer. He said he started sleeping in the guest wing because he didn't wish to wake me, coming in during the late hours from working. But I am not so sure any longer. Do you think he wishes he had not married me?

Nothing I can do about it now, though, is there? I have made my bed and I must lay in it, even if I lay in it alone. I just thought he loved me so much and now I am not so sure what he feels. But he does want me to go with him to Buffalo, and that is something.

Perhaps this summer I can come for a visit. That would be so much fun. I will see what I can do and perhaps we will be able to spend some time together. I think it would do my heart a wonder of good.

Give my love to your husband and your family. I shall write back as soon as I return from the Exposition and tell you all the wonderful details.

All my love,
Maggie

7 July, 1901

My Dearest Cousin Rachel,

Please forgive my late return of your post. I have been so consumed by the happenings here that I scarcely find time to catch my own breath. I had never before realized just how much Father managed until now. I only ever considered his legal practice but I now fully understand his diversity. Father was such a wonderful and brilliant man, I only wish he had a son to entrust this to. I have no mind for business. And you would think Artie would help me or take charge in my stead, but he refuses. I have found that Mrs. Rutherford seems to have much less to say to me of late, as well. A fine person she is to snub me with insinuations of a wife's and mother's place, too. Why, she is the very person who would argue on and on about how women should be running businesses and making money of their own. I even recall her enthusiasm for women to get the vote and chastising me for being backward and not nearly so progressive as herself.

She says I should sell out all those business partnerships and the like that Father left me and settle back down to be a proper wife. I also notice that I have received a great many offers to buy my inheritance, too. People I have never heard of or scarcely recall meeting once at a dinner party are falling from the eaves. I may not know the true value of most of this, but I can certainly see false sympathy and hear a forked tongue. I have been approached by more business men than you can believe, all expressing their deep regrets at the loss of my father and designing their attempt to steal our family fortune as their way of helping me past this grieving period. After all, I do not need the added frustrations of attending to everything Father left behind. I am just a woman, after all.

I have begun to feel a bit more progressive than I ever thought I would. The funny thing is that I could have lived my whole life as Artie's wife and the mother of his children, happily by his side and supporting him in every way possible, but I find I truly do not like being treated as though I am incapable of anything else.

What is more, Artie seems to be completely bullish about the whole affair. It appears, now that it comes to it, that Father was worth much, much more than anyone realized, including Artie. I think he and his family thought of my family as a bit lower class than they. I had always felt it, though I preferred not to mention it. I think it is because they have always been so happy to flaunt their wealth.

Well, I never went without anything at all and by all means, Father never spared an expense when I wanted something. However, we have never been like the Rutherfords. You would never catch Mrs. Rutherford helping in the sick tents during the epidemics. And Mother never had a servant to follow her about with a parasol through town. In fact, the ladies who worked in our home were always treated more like family. You should see the way Artie's parents treat their household. I brought Nanna with me to their house once, after Little Artie was born, and Mrs. Rutherford had a tempered fit when Nanna and I sat at the garden together. At that time I still felt so unnerved by Mrs. Rutherford, I did not know what to do. Nanna, bless her, told me not to worry and she went into the kitchen.

Perhaps that is the difference. The Rutherfords are greatly concerned with everyone else knowing they are the wealthiest family. Of course, that is absurd. There is always someone wealthier. In fact, that is just the problem. With all their beautiful things and snobbish aire, bossing everyone else about and making them feel they have to put up with it, they suddenly find out in a rather embarrassing way, that they are not as above me as they thought. They looked down on me and my whole family. I cannot believe how silly I was. I allowed myself to feel so inferior to them. At least I was contented with my family. In fact, I always thought my father was a far better man than any of them and I was correct. Not because he had more money, but because no one even realized he had it.

Oh, I know, everyone knew we had plenty of money. I am not trying to suggest otherwise, simply that a loud mouth does not necessarily make you right or in control. And that brings me to something else. While these pandering men come about attempting to buy my inheritance for a fraction of its worth, they lather their offers with such flattering respect, pretending to speak to me as an equal. It makes my stomach burn like hot coals to think of it.

There was one, just this past week, who came by to discuss purchasing Father's interest in a railroad. He could barely conceal the smile I caught almost flickering across his face as he spoke to me. I caught straight away that he was using phrases and words he thought would confuse me, in fact, he intended it to do so. Have you ever heard of a strumfiggler? No, I am sure you have not. I never have. And do you know why? Because it is not a word at all. Yet that man, Parsons I believe was his name, sat in my parlor and with a face of stone told me that the strumfiggler reports did not look well and that the whole situation could go awry at any time and he would certainly understand if I wanted to get out and, because of the unfortunate circumstances I am faced with, he would agree to help me. How kind of him, do you agree?

And does Artie do anything to help me? No. He completely refuses to give me any advice whatsoever. He will not explain anything to me. I would happily hand it all over to him to manage, but he says it is my inheritance and I should do with it as I see fit. It is as if he hopes I will be duped into losing it all.

Oh, Rachel, I am so afraid that is what will eventually happen, too. There are so many things. There are all kinds of properties, hotels, businesses, railroad and even something to do with the telephone and automobiles. It looks like Father had his hand in half the businesses in town in some way or another. I always knew he carried considerable influence and received a great deal of respect from people wherever we went, but I did not understand the extent of it. I just wish he had better prepared me for this. I am sure he thought Artie would be of much more use. No wonder he felt Artie would a good husband for me. He knew that Artie had been preened to take over a considerable amount of his father's investments. It makes so much sense now.

Rachel, am I wrong? I cannot make myself throw away

all these things that Father worked so much to provide. He left this entrusted to me and I so want for it to be Little Artie's some day. But how? Perhaps all these circling vultures are right. Maybe a woman isn't meant for this much.

I remember when Artie and I were courting and he would sit in the parlor and discuss politics and tell me about all these incredible things. I thought he must be the smartest man in the world and it flattered me so much that he found me worthy to discuss these things with, even though I understood so little of what he said. I danced with my head in the clouds, but I fear they are firmly on the ground now.

I do not know what to do. I think I shall speak to Mr. Baker this coming week. Father always trusted him and I think, perhaps, I should trust in Father's faith. Mr. Baker has never made me feel foolish or inadequate. I must say he has been patient and taken time to explain things to me when I ask questions. Perhaps he would make the best counselor. I believe, if anyone does, he will know what Father's intentions were.

I must not forget, the Exposition was quite intriguing. I wish you were there with me. There were some women there with minds for business. Very successful women. But it was absolutely fabulous. The lights burned brilliant and so beautiful, I can hardly explain it. They looked astonishingly like the sunset. Everything was large and grand. The gardens were simply lovely and the booths were all so interesting.

We met the vice president and his wife, a remarkable woman in her own way, certainly not shy at all. I wish I had been able to spend a little more time with Artie. What can I say, though? He spent more time with his assistant than with his son or me. I cannot say what it is about the man that troubles me, but something does. I almost feel jealous, but that is silly. I might as well be jealous of Artie's work. He does work too much, though. He comes in late in the night. I sometimes sit at the uppermost steps and listen for him to arrive. I hear the door open and close, then his footsteps tapping his way up to the guest wing. I miss him. Perhaps that is one reason I do not wish to give up Father's businesses too hastily. I need something more. I no longer feel like a real wife. It is as though I have served my purpose, supplied an heir, a son, and now it is my tasteful responsibility to host tea and be charming upon demand. It is such an empty feeling.

Perhaps all wives feel like this sometimes. I do not know. Without Mother to ask, it is difficult to say and who else is there? You are the only person I can trust. We both know our aunts are not adept to keeping a secret. People love to gossip about us already. If anyone found out that we no longer share our sleeping quarters, I think I would simply die of embarrassing shame. And I know there would be a hefty number of women eager to replace my side of the bed if they could get a chance. No, I think I shall just have to wonder and pray this is just a passing chapter in our lives.

I am becoming weary. I think I shall attempt to sleep. Artie has still not come home, but who knows when he will. I am enclosing a few things I brought home from the Exposition I wanted you to see. I am hoping for good news from you soon. Give my love to everyone.

Love always,
Maggie

1 September, 1901

Dearest Cousin Rachel,

The hours grow late once again. Little Artie is asleep in my bed. He looks so beautiful and sweet. Arthur, as he now prefers to be called in public, came home about an hour ago and I went downstairs to greet him. I have seen so little of him recently. He comes in quite late every night and it seems the only time we spend together is our arrival at Sunday services. Of course, he will not miss that, he is far too worried about appearances and maintaining his respectable image. Yet, it is not as if we speak to one another then; that would be improper. On occasion, when the need is too great, I go to his office, but not too often.

I am not a jealous woman, but my heart has been darkened with the thought that there may be another woman. I am well aware of the rumors about his father and his mistresses. I feel there must be something wrong and I wonder what I can do to make everything right again. Even if there is no mistress, he certainly finds no use for me. Many women might be glad of this, but I am not. I would like to have another child. You always seemed so happy with your sister. I wanted that same kind of happiness for little Artie. I would dearly love for him to have a brother or sister he could always look to and grow up with. I never had a sibling, but always envied others who did.

Yes, I did enjoy being Father's little girl, but still, I think I would rather to have shared his affection and have a brother or sister who would still be with me. It is quite lonely to have no close family. I fear if I cannot find a way to change my husband's heart, then poor little Artie will suffer the same lonely fate when both his father and I have passed.

Perhaps you may think of some way for me to win Arthur's affection once more. I fear he no longer loves me. To be honest with myself, I fear he never did. But then why would he marry me? He was so charming and I love him so much. But were it all a lie, how could I carry on? Mother and Father loved each other so, and I always thought marriage must be such, yet here I find that it is not always so. If I am not now the woman he loves, do you think I can make myself into someone he admires? Admiration is not love, but it is better than indifference.

There is more sad news as well. It seems Nanna is

growing ill. I know she is quite old, though even she cannot say quite how many years. She tries to hide her sickness, but I keep a close eye on her. She is taking tonic morning and night but she still must rest in the midday. I have Veronica, my chief housemaid, look in on her and take her tea. Nanna has earned the right to pampering more than any person I can imagine. She has been with my family all her life and her mother and father before her. I asked her many times when I was young why she never married and she told me that this family was enough to be getting on with and she didn't need no more work. That made me laugh when I was a child, yet now, it makes me sad to recall. Dear Nanna gave up a family of her own to take care of ours. Can such love and loyalty be rewarded with a wage? Nanna is the grandmother I never knew and the mother I lost.

Artie thinks I am too sentimental and claims Nanna has only done as a servant is meant to do. As with everything, he is cold and distant. I wonder if there is anything that he ever truly loved. If Nanna passes, then I know I will feel so absolutely alone. Little Artie is all that I have close to me. His father has no time for either of us and I find I must interrupt his work at his office in order to speak to him at all. He always appears so pleasant and loving in the presence of his colleagues, though slightly indulging, but his temperament changes so when we find ourselves alone. I say alone, but we hardly ever are that. Mr. Durham, Bill Durham, Arthur's assistant, never seems to leave Arthur's side. Even private and personal conversations, Artie does not send him away. The more I see the man, the less I like him. It is the queerest thing, the way he looks at me. I fear he is capable of some sort of scandal, but how could I ever express this to Artie? He simply will not hear a word against the man.

And would you believe that Artie, in some peculiar change of heart regarding my father's businesses, suggested that if I wouldn't sell the lot, that he could set

Mr. Darhman to manage it all. I truly loath that man. I see something indecent in his eyes and I do not trust him in the least. No, I would rather squander everything than allow that scoundrel to defile my father's work. But I am learning more about Father's business most every day and the funniest thing has happened over all this time of indecision, nothing. It all runs itself. There are people who seem to do all the work and I only oversee a few things here and there, just to keep the employees honest. I had wondered how Father had time to practice law with so many investments. For some reason, I have not conveyed this discovery to Arthur, though. Perhaps I am still hoping that he will want to take care of it for me, shelter me from all the goings of the world. But his offer for Mr. Darhman was no such ploy of rescue, but an overture which displayed that same look of greed and bilk I had seen in the dozens who attempted to steal my assets in the weeks before.

I feel a terrible burning inside me when I think of these things. What kind of wife am I? I would gladly give all of everything I have to Artie, but not to that man, not to Darhman. But how can I think that my husband would have me swindled? Yet how can I believe otherwise? My heart is so confused. Here I lay my troubles and worries out to you, as if you haven't enough of your own, but I have no one else to confide these fears. I surely miss the days and hours we spent whispering in secret our hopes and dreams, but those memories grow darker and seem far away. But not all is sad. I have my little one and he cheers me beyond measure.

Oh, I do hope to hear from you soon. It lightens my heart and you always have the best insight. Give my love to your family.

Truly yours,
Maggie

3 November, 1901

Dearest Rachel,

Oh Rachel, I am so happy to hear the wonderful news. Your letter met me in poor spirits, but as always, you have cheered my heart beyond measure. A baby is so exciting and wonderful. Though I do hope you will be careful. I cannot forget the months and months you spent ill and bedridden. Please take care to let others do for you when they can. You will need your strength.

But I must insist on many a visit soon. I would like to be there when you birth. I am sure you will have ample help to tend you, however, I have learned that too much service can prove more hindrance than help. If you may recall my sullen melancholy? A mother must be allowed to fulfill those tasks our divine Creator intended, lest we deprive our soul the joys of motherhood

My only fear is that my business might interfere with any plans to travel abroad. I now underhand Father so much better than I ever did during his life. It required such admirable strength and wisdom to enact such discipline to maintain, even grow, his wealth. I have learned so much.

Difficult as it may be to believe, I have grown into a new person. While I am always first, Artie's mother, I have also become a business woman. I found that I can the both. True, I must devote considerable time to business affairs, but there is time for both. Arthur never intended for my success. When we courted, I felt astounded when he asked my opinion on any trivial matter. His mother always spoke of progress and women's right to achieve success. I spent long hours forced to endure the opinions regarding her infinite hypocrisy. She felt Arthur deserved a wife with the composure to look to the future, encouraging acceptance of women in both business and politics. Yet now, after so long declaring my frailty and delicate manners as a hindrance to my husband, she now proclaims that his change of affection results from my brazen attempts to act the part of a man, disgracing him publicly. She certainly entertains some bravado, suggesting now that I should behave less independent and more like the traditional, devoted wife our social class should be. I do not believe she ever meant a word of that progressive ideology. I look at her now and it is as though I have only just seen her. You see, she is neither what she so devoutly supported, nor what she claims she wants to change. Alas, poor Mrs. Rutherford is a victim of her wealth. Servants robbed her of motherhood and the need to tend her house. Mistresses replaced her as a beloved wife. She possessed no inherent skills of her own to pursue. All the boisterous and ever-aging Mrs. Rutherford could hold as her own was her relentless ideology. Now I fear she believes I have stolen that as well. Worse, even still, I have become a testimonial to the truth she spoke, albeit never believed.

I fear she may never forgive me for proving her right, though the honesty I hold secret in my heart cannot deny feeling a small amount of pleasure at my dear mother-in-law's anguish. I cannot ever forget her snobbish demeanor when first Artie and I courted nor these subsequent years. She always wanted me to feel inferior. Now I realize she felt threatened by me. But enough of this. Enough of her for all her lectures I endured, it was not she whom inspired me to become something more. The catapult of my adventure. I thank my brooding husband for that. I know what you would say and you are correct. He offered no help whatsoever, There was no inspiration, not a single word of hope, confidence or even advice. Unless you count that dubious offer to allow his wretched assistant run his filthy hands through my fathers fortune. No. He wanted me to fail. I saw it in his face, the way he twisted his smile with contempt. I just could not succumb to his loathing. It sparked something down in the deep of my breast that simply refused to allow me to give in to him. Remember, I did not want a progressive life.

And now I think I finally understand his displeasure. It

seems that Arthur fancied Father would name him as his heir, being married to me. He never suspected that Father would circumvent him, or worse, require him to answer to me for his actions where my inheritance was concerned. Apparently, Father insulted him, created a public issue of trust and impugned his character by the actions of his will.

Who knew one could do so much from the grave? Once I join Father in heaven, I must thank him. For now, my prayers must convey that message.

Oh which does bring my heart back to the tragedy. Can you believe President McKinley assassinated? It stills my heart. In turn it has proven to make business uncertain for a time. I never realized the role politics plays in the working of investments, and I now see it is no wonder men discussed it so often. I fear I will be forced to endure learning this as well.

It seems once again I have rambled on and on about my problems. At least I am slowly arriving at answers. I enjoy learning Father's business. I finally appreciate the education he insisted upon, for without it, I would have quickly been swindled many times. The affairs of money proves a ruthless game.

I do envy you. All I ever wanted, a husband, home and children, is what you have. True, I have little Artie and would exchange him for naught, but I always thought mine would be the home of little padding footsteps, tinkling laughter and hours upon glorious hours of play. I wanted a large family and it is apparent now that it is not to be.

Matters, I fear, have not changed regards to my relationship with Arthur, I assume you guessed as much from my earlier revelations.

I have looked at myself again and again and cannot discern anything significantly changed. I even went so far as to inquire to his mother about his behavior. I attempted to allure' him as you suggested. Oh, it was so terrible. You cannot believe the complete humiliation. His lip curled into snarl and an expression of complete disgust-burned in his eyes. He simply finds the idea of marital relations with me repulsive. His mother had a most peculiar reaction, at least initially . Horror. Absolutely nothing short of horror gripped her entire body. She clenched her tea so hard, it tipped, then she dropped it, cup, saucer and all. Tea drenched her napkin and the tablecloths. It took several moments for her to gain her composure and even then, I found her words strange. First she questioned about whether I suspected a mistress and advised that if he had taken one that I should still never consider divorce. The scandal would the devastating for everyone. She also told me of Mr. Rutherford's multiple indiscretions. Surprised, I certainly questioned why she would remain with someone so frightfully disloyal. She laughed, a very nervous laugh, that left me uneasy. She said for people of our station, loyalty was not measured by a man's ability to remain faithful, but in that you alone provide the heir to his fortune: Remaining the lady of the house was a great reward.

I told her I did not believe he had a mistress. Then she looked most disheartened. It seemed she hoped he had some scarlet woman somewhere. But then she questioned, carefully I noted, why I felt so.

I explained that it appeared he seldom even left the company of that employee of his. In fact, he frequently takes a room in the guest wing as well. Arthur says it is only courteous because of the hours he devotes to Arthur, but something does not sit well about the matter.

At that point, Mrs. Rutherford appeared to set herself in resolve. She then blamed my Father and me for bringing this unhappiness on her son. This is when I discovered that Father had shamed Arthur publicly by his unconventional determination of his will. And then, of course, she blamed me for not simply liquidating my assets immediately, knowing my husband could not play an ass, working for his wife. At that point, I politely excused myself from tea. I told her I had a business engagement I must attend to, But still, I think something important was said, or perhaps not said, but somehow inspired in our discussion.

My hand grows weary, but I loath to stop. Writing to you is my only chance to express how I feel. I do not get to spend as much time with little Artie as I would like. I find if I spend too long apart from my dearest little one, then my heart aches, yet I must fulfill obligations required of a business owner.

I have had a thought Yes. I still have the literature from The World Fair. I kept it as souvenirs, however it may have some information to help. Well, it wont help with my beloved husband, but perhaps I could better learn how to manage being both mother and entrepreneur.

As for all else, I know not what has befallen me. The new power I hold thrills me, but I think it a poor substitute for the arms of my husband and marriage. I have no wish to choose. In that, at least, Mrs. Rutherford is correct. I cannot dishonor all my family or myself. I simply wish upon wish that something would clear this haze of uncertainty. If Arthur no longer desires to share a bed with me, forgive my forward language, then I would appreciate knowing why. A gnawing seed of failure is pitted in my stomach.

Here I am melancholy once more. How dour of me. Especially when you have given me the best of news. You have hoped for this for so long and my joy rings out to you. Please do be careful. Your wellness means so much to me. Now, how selfish is that? I truly am a spoiled child. But none the less, I depend on your letters to keep me grounded. After little Artie, you are the most cherished person in my life. I had best put an end to this ceaseless drabble of my life. At the least I do hope you find my ridiculous ramble amusing. Give my love to all and once again, watch your health.

Truly yours,
Maggie

CHAPTER FIVE: 1902

1 January, 1902

Dearest Cousin Rachel,

My dear, sweet family and friend, I wish we were close once more. I miss so much the way things once were, as it was in our youth. I long for our lives before this charade of promises when we dreamed about life and love. We shared such a beautiful time. Life has not made the turns I anticipated. When I received your letter, it filled my heart with wonderful gladness. But I fear there is nothing that can mend this torture that has now gripped my soul. I have not the words to explain the travesty that has befallen my home. It is beyond words and shall certainly never be uttered aloud, not even in the most secret of places, not even in the lonely silence of my bedroom when all else are sleeping. It is that formidable and that terrible. I have discovered a secret, a terrible truth and there is no one but you, my sweet cousin and dearest friend, that I feel I can trust. I have never felt so alone nor so angry and deceived in my life. The anger is not just for me, but for sweet little Arlie as well. It seems such a shame that my only child and the truest love in my heart must share a befouled name with that indecent louse. A woman should feel ashamed to speak such a way about her husband, yet all I feel is a deep disgust and betrayal.

I know you do not understand. There is no way that you could. My heart is convulsive with grief and despair, attempting to understand myself. But who could know such a thing?

Last night we held our New Year Celebration, as has become our custom. I wore the most wonderful dark green gown with cascades of crushed velvet and true emeralds set about the bust. Lovell's spent near four months of preparation to complete such a wondrous creation. Being the hostess of such functions I have learned requires that I dress the most lavish, laugh the most often and appear almost dizzy with joy and happiness. Mother taught me such and it has proven true. How I wish she were here to help me now. I fear I would not dare to tell even Father such a terrible thing. The shame is beyond what my mortal being can endure.

But, returning to the party, I wanted to look beautiful. Not merely for our guests, but I thought perhaps I could entice Arthur. The loss of his affection has tormented me. I hoped that if I looked beautiful enough, perhaps I could enchant his interests once more. A childish and romantic thought, I know, but still, my desperation drove me. It is so difficult to explain. I do not know how I could so easily have allowed my heart to be misguided. For that, I know not who holds the true fault, him or me.

The party went lovely, as it always does. Arthur seemed more affectionate than he has of late and I felt sure my plan had worked. I allowed my heart to feel a shadow of joy and excitement. I wanted so much for him to love me. Is that wrong? I wanted my husband to love me. I wanted him to hold me and tell me he would protect me from the world. That is a security no purse can buy.

But perhaps my hopes clouded my vision. For it is clear he harbors no love for me and perhaps never has. I wish I knew if I had ever held his love or if our courtship and marriage were nothing more than play to protect his and the Rutherford's family names.

Oh, dear Rachel, what I found is so terrible. I know not how to say it and I find myself, even within my letter to you, stalling at every measure, trying to avoid a truth so noxious I feel I may suffocate at any moment.

After the guests left, spurred by my feelings and a flush of wine, I asked Arthur to come to my room, our room. The soft expression he had worn all evening dissolved into a wretched, cold malice. He did not even answer. But turned to that infernal man, Mr. Durham, and said he was retiring and suggested that he do the same soon. Then told him that he should remain at our house in the usual quarters we have provided. I believe I told you before, but Arthur has afforded Mr. Durham a sweet in the guest wing near the rooms Arthur keeps. He said at the time Bill and he worked so closely and such long hours that it was a matter of convenience. Of course, I believed him, although my dislike for the awful little man did not improve with ever-closer proximity.

My husband scarcely acknowledged me with a rise of his chin and walked away, leaving me in the dining hall, embarrassed, confused and boiling with anger. How could he simply dismiss me as he would a servant? And to treat me thus in the company of that little serpent. Oh, you should have seen the little snickering grin he gave me. That should have said all I needed to know, yet I still found myself in the dark.

After storming to my dressing room, I told Nanna what had occurred. I have tried to keep most of my worries to myself simply because of her poor health. I know she would feel responsible for my happiness. I just could not jeopardize her confronting Arthur and the conflict ending in her dismissal. But I fear my anger and hurt could not be disguised and I found myself sobbing into her lap while she listened and stroked my hair. It seems, looking back, that even she could not foresee the terrible truth.

Had I not spoken with Nanna, I would not know what I now know. She encouraged me to march up to his room and demand his attention. So, bolstered by her strength and conviction, I washed my face and made the tedious walk to Arthur's room. My strength began to fail about midway and it took all my effort to continue. I think my heart must already have known its destiny, for it ached in my chest with each step I took. I heard their voices at the edge of the hall. A high pitched, giggling laugh rung out, echoing in the arched antechamber as I approached. My breath left me as I realized Arthur was not alone. He appeared to be entertaining some scarlet woman and in our very home. My heartbreak seethed into fury and I flung the doors wide open. I wanted no mistake. I shall refuse to live in willful darkness. He will not play host to his tramp lover in my home.

I thought I could endure no more heartache, embarrassment or shame, yet what I found exceeded anything I have ever felt. Should this secret ever escape, it would certainly ruin our lives. Now I am forced to live with a terrible shame for the sake of my son. If this were found out, it would surely devour his life. So please, I implore you, I plead even though I know I need not, let no one ever know what I tell you. I have told no one else, not even Nanna when I retuned to my bed, both alone and ashen with shock. Then I forbade her to ever ask of me or Arthur what had occurred. I have never given her such a command before and she knew well not to try me on it.

There in Arthur's bedchamber I found them. Their naked bodies entwined with one another in such a way as there to be no mistaking their actions. I discovered Arthur and his lover, but Lord help us, Rachel, his lover is Bill. He has taken himself with another man. Perhaps I have led a sheltered life, I am sure that I have. But this is beyond my knowledge. I feel so confused. I am angry with him yet I feel guilty and ashamed. How terrible a wife must I be for this to happen.

I cannot forget their faces, their eyes, when they saw me standing there. Arthur wore an expression of terror while Bill, Mr. Durham, quickly moved from shock to satisfaction.

The images are haunting and evil. I cannot, will not say what Mr. Durham then did, but I feet a violent sickness emerge and 1 turned, grasping the doorframe and wretched, Then without looking back, I ran through the corridors to my bedroom, called for the nurse to bring Little Artie to my chanters and then leave us.

I could see the worry on Nanna's face, but I quickly forbade her to ask of it. She looked hurt, but this is one family secret that she need not know.

So there. Now I have told you and my energy is spent. I do not know who else I can turn to. I thought of our priest, but then what would happen? I need your advice desperately. I truly feel orphaned now. I have not left my rooms today, neither has Artie . I sent for our meals to be served here, Arthur has made no attempt to speak with me. Were it not winter and unbearable to attempt the journey, I would consider this an excellent time to visit you or make a trip abroad. We shall see.

Oh, I must stop here. My heart fails and I need rest. I apologize for disclosing such a terrible thing to you during what should be the happiest time. Please forgive me. I shall await your response.

All my love,
Maggie

27 February, 1902

Dearest Rachel,

It is so wonderful to hear! A daughter. I know she is certainly beautiful. I love the name you have chosen.

Elizabeth Carlita. It sounds exotic and almost mystical. I know you and your husband are so proud. You deserve such happiness. Be mindful of your rest, though. It is so important to maintain your strength.

I am also grateful for your kindness. I have not made any rash decisions. In fact, I have really done nothing at all. Mr. Durham has not been to the house since that terrible night. I can the thankful for some small favors.

The truth is that Arthur and I have not spoken a single word. We have breakfast the same as always, though he seldom looks up at me aside for short glances. Yet I can find myself completely forgetting my food and simply staring at him for many long moments at a time. But though I watch him, I still cannot find words. My throat feels swollen and my tongue too thick to move. More often than not, I send my plates away scarcely touched.

It has taken a toll upon my health, for all my clothes are becoming loose. I know I must not allow myself to waste with grief. Little Artie needs me. You are right and you know me so well. But you need not worry nor chide. I promise to do better from now forward.

If I must, I shall have additional meals brought to my room. I do not know why, but I feel I must continue meeting for breakfast if Arthur is here. Some semblance of normalcy must remain for the sake of our son. I pray every night and morning that he never finds out about his father's perversion. For what else could I call it?

For now, I know not how else to deal with such a circumstance.

But as for you, I shall hear no such worries. You will make a wonderful mother. You are an incredible lady. And by far the bravest woman I have over known. Just think of all you have done. You left our childhood home for the Western Hope. Then you traveled farther still after wedding such a kind man. You took his residence in another country. If you can brave all this, you certainly can face motherhood. Just keep your strength and I promise, even when all else in the world may feel lost, you will always feel in your heart what you must do for your little one. This I know. All too well I fear. I think you shall be the most wonderful mother in all the world. When I look at all the times I have cried to you and with such patience, you always new what to say. You are both kind and honest, qualities I fear are becoming less and less common. So trust me, if only this one time. You are a wonderful mother and you offer your daughter the best teacher in the world, no matter what cultural differences there may be.

Little Artie has grown so. He will be a young man before long. Time is deceitful. Was it not just last month he lay in my arms as an infant? Now he runs about, terrorizing the whole house. I must soon decide some course of action, I do not wish these problems between Arthur and I to affect poor little Artie. He is a smart lad and I see he already senses something is wrong.

If only I knew what to do. The situation seems so hopeless. And I believe Mrs. Rutherford knew of this peculiarity all along, or at least suspected it. But enough of this. It wears on my heart.

Nanna has taken ill. She tries to hide it, but I can see the evidence more and more. She has lived some long years, though she cannot, or will not, say just how many. And it is not as though she cannot count. Grandfather insisted that she learn arithmetic and reading. It is a great source of pride for her and always has been. She's told me so many times how proud her mother was for her child to learn her numbers and letters. Though, between you and me, Nanna's reading has been a bit out of practice for a while. But she enjoys reading little stories to Artie. I do, too.

That has made me think, what language will you teach your child? They speak Spanish in Mexico, is that right? But does that mean your children should learn Spanish? I realize you have had to learn much of the language simply to run the house, but is that enough? I am not sure how I would communicate if my child spoke another language than I do. But then again, I often feel that way. Most of what he says is incoherent, anyway!

I apologize, I do not mean to upset you, but I am most curious. I suppose she could learn both English and Spanish. It seems taxing, but given her circumstance, it might be most useful.

I feel tired. As I said, recent events have brutalized my health. I shall end for now. Please send all my love to your family. I know they are most excited about the birth of your daughter. Please keep yourself rested and healthy. I shall look for the most splendid gift now that she is born. I await your next letter with an eager heart. And give your darling husband my congratulations. I know he must be to proud. May God bless you all and keep you safe.

Truly yours,
Maggie

25 April, 1902

Dearest Cousin Rachel,

Your letter arrived just days ago and I have read it many times. I ache for the loneliness you feel, but wish to reassure you. I cannot believe your darling husband has any interest outside of your arms. When you and he came to visit, the mere expression of this gaze when his dark eyes fell upon you spoke of an incredible love. No one could ever forsake such a vow of their heart. It would cripple his soul. I truly believe you worry for naught.

I know you feel a distance from him since Carlita's birth, but know, dear cousin, that it is to be expected. A man must learn to share his wife, even when his competitor is someone as precious as his child. You say he does dote over her and to see him so happy with her warms your heart. So take peace with that and know this is just the way of things. It shall right itself soon enough.

And know, too, if he is not lurking upon you every absent moment, you will recover all the quicker. There is something practical in the nature of things.

You need not fear anything so terrible as my plot, I feel ashamed now, knowing your fragile state, at having confided so much of my problems. It has given you too much to consider and now you see shadows of deceit about you. For that, I accept my rightful blame. I did not mean to be so conceited, for my grief was truly founded. But take heart, for I know that yours is not.

Yet, I think I can make you feel somewhat better. For Arthur and I finally spoke to one another. He came to my bedroom one evening after supper and Artie had been put to bed. We had all supped together, a silent wall erected between us that even little Artie dared not to disturb.

When he entered, I saw a terrible look of pain upon his face. It differed so from his usual sneer of contempt that I felt my heart sway for a moment. But only a moment, mind. That is all it took to become overwhelmed by the hideous memory scarred upon my heart. But still, there was one moment where my heart stirred and I wanted to love him once more.

But can that ever be?

He came to tell me that Mr. Durham would not be retuning to the estate and that he also was no longer in Arthur's employ.

I could see he felt pained by this. Do you think Arthur really cared for this deviant? I had accepted that Arthur must suffer from some perverted illness, but could it be more? Is there more to this than some wicked desire that captures his heat as well? What of love?

I fear my heart could not take a deception so conceived. Do you think I should worry for little Artie? Could this nature become inherited, from father to son? I know not how to discourage such a thing. But then I think of Mrs. Rutherford and I understand that I would love my precious son no matter.

I did manage to ask him the reason. He sat on the settee and appeared near tears. The show of emotion unsettled me all the more. Yet he managed to restrain himself and preserve what little dignity remains to him. Before he began to speak, his eyes bore into the wall, as though seeing something I could not. Such behavior in one I always thought so strong stung my heart. I felt that I, at that moment, had only just seen his true self. But he went on to say that given recent events and the unexpected revelation of certain circumstances, Mr. Durham had requested that he be allowed unrestricted access to our estate.

Of course, I have tried to tell you word for word as best I can manage, and I feel certain you will agree that his words were quite confusing. And yes, dear Rachel, I most certainly did ask him what on earth that meant.

Then he explained, less formally, that Mr. Durham wanted to live at our estate, since I came to know of their relationship.

I believe my heart truly leapt into my throat. My eyes and ears burned and the very breath in my bosom drained away. I do not exaggerate, but truly say, I felt myself sway, near faint.

Arthur swept me into his arms before I collapsed to the floor and lifted me into a chair. I feel almost ashamed to admit that for the briefest moment, he looked heroic once more. But too quickly the moment passed and he withdrew again.

I tried to utter something, wanting assurance that his first announcement, declaring the ghastly man would not return was true. Arthur answered my silent plea, saying when he refused Mr. Durham his request, that he threatened Arthur with ending the affair and leaving his employ. Arthur told him, "if you must." And so it ended.

Arthur then apologized for the pain he has caused me and said he would understand if I sought to have our marriage put away, though he did not desire to shame me, his son or his family with divorce. He then stood and left my quarters. I watched him leave, but could not say a word. At that moment I both loved and hated him with every drop of life within me.

I have no intention of requesting a divorce from Arthur. Though, given the circumstances, the church might allow it. I have no wish to stain my son with his father's sins. No one else must know of this, even if the secret were to drain my life away. I must protect my son.

Perhaps these wounds will not prove mortal and eventually heal. We have, at the least, spoken. That must be a step down the path.

But you have enough to worry with now, and here I find myself forever confiding in you. Would that I had but one trusted friend here, then perhaps you could be spared the brunt of my strife. You are too kind a friend.

In brighter news, business is going quite well. Mr. Baker says I have done an excellent job and I have an incredibly intuitive head, as well as beautiful. He says that is a dangerous mix. Of course, he merely teases me so. Though we have seen an excellent profit margin in the last year. Would you ever have thought to hear such words from me? I have grown more confident. But there is not too much to worry over. Though I am considering selling my share of the Grand Hotel. For some reason, it just doesn't make the money it should considering how much is invested. I may take a closer look at why before I sell it, though. I cannot believe I sit and think about things like this now. I never thought myself bright enough and certainly not capable as a modern businesswoman. It amazes me, the incredible faith Father showed, but also makes me wonder if he did not suspect something amiss with Arthur from the beginning. This marriage was thought to combine estates, but not with my generation. It shall be little Artie who holds that scepter.

I shall close now, that you may take some rest from my problems. Remember you have nothing to worry about.

Your husband loves you beyond compare. I envy his devotion to you. So bring cheer to your heart and rejoice in the beautiful life you brought forth.

Give my love to the family.

Very truly yours,
Maggie

22 July, 1902

Dearest Cousin Rachel,

It is wonderful to hear your problems with Miguel are resolved. I knew your had nothing to fear. He is a wonderful and romantic man with eyes only for you. It is such a beautiful bond of love laced with pearls of passion. A precious mantle that drapes the two of you. Have I said before how much I envy you? And do not think it is only I. Oh, I still hear the ladies speak in town about you and your Latin prince charming. As he passed down our streets, he swept the women off their feet with his masculine charm and radiant manner. But they merely fell to the ground, awoken by the dust, for your hand was the only he would take and his black eyes, like liquid night, they saw only you. Poetic, perhaps, but it certainly entertained me for quite a long time. In fact, your visit, and Miguel in specific, frequently rises to the height of chattering at Lovelle's.

Though you were perhaps unaware, but Miss Penelope Jones felt certain she could gain his affections. Always one for trouble, she is. Her family has had one right difficult time with her. It seems she would prefer to take a gentleman betrothed rather than properly court and marry with honor. You know the girl, but she was simply a child when you left here. She is certainly not a child any longer and if they do not find a fitting suitor soon, she may find herself in a brothel. I fear she is just the type; very beautiful and enjoys exhibiting a flirtatious personality. At times, her behavior is simply uncouth and unacceptable.

The point is that she made her best play for Miguel when he and the other men were out one evening, and your wonderful man excused her from his presence in a most demeaning manner. She ran from the place in tears while Miguel simply returned to his conversation and drink, as though nothing had occurred at all.

Oh, perhaps you have already heard that story. But it is still a favorite one while being fitted at Lovell's. So all the women here think of Miguel and sigh, wishing their own prince could feel so much for them as that.

There was once a time the women envied me, too. And though I have said nothing to convey any distress in our home, it appears rumors have still bled out, yet, it could be much worse. I hear whisper that Arthur is a philanderer just as his father. Oh dear, I have only had this thought come upon me. His father has such a reputation for keeping mistresses. Could it be a rouse to disguise something altogether more different?

I had found myself almost grateful that he be considered an adulterer. The truth would destroy our lives altogether. The Church is set against such a life.

Arthur and I have spoken at length now. We both agree that no one should be told anything about what happened. We plan to keep on hire any of the house staff that could perhaps have deduced the nature of Arthur and Mr. Durham's relationship for as long as possible. Thus we can maintain a measure of control over them. Our worst fear is that Mr. Durham will seek retribution by slandering Arthur or even turn to blackmail.

But to avoid such accusations, Arthur and 1 will return to sleeping in the same quarters. We even discussed the possibility of having another child, though I have not yet accepted that proposal.

I do not want a divorce. And I know that Arthur hopes to enter politics soon. But even though I have longed for another child, wished upon wishes to make it so, I simply am not yet prepared to engage in that sort of intimacy with Arthur again. There was a time, and not so long ago, that I called him Artie. I felt a flock of fluttering butterflies swirl through any stomach each time he took my hand. But now, those feelings have been replaced.

Now, when he takes my hand, I am overcome by an ebb of illness. It washes over me, leaving my face pale, my breath shallow and my stomach twisted. I know not how a child can be conceived in such way. For this reason , I feel we must wait. However I understand my years for childbirth are nearing an end. It should be soon. I have seen women in their mid and late twenties bring forth children, but too often, the childbirth takes them. I cannot afford to leave little Artie without a mother to help him through some very difficult and confusing times ahead. Yet Arthur believes that should we have another child now, it would make the perfect way to disprove any allegations regarding our marriage. Practical, yes, as always. But I'm afraid I need more than practical to convince me he has changed this habit and will not have a relapse that could destroy us all.

Now, I do sound so full of cheer. Better news, my business is looking wonderful I have hired an assistant, Peter Floyd, to help with general affairs. He is a smart man and I believe my father would approve.

The real reason in choosing a man is simple, although I did feel pressured by the Association for Ladies in Business, a rather unique group of progressive ladies who have found themselves interested in me. They are somehow connected with the organization I attended with the Vice President's wife I think two years passed. When we attended the World Fair. In any event, they were the fist to suggest that I hire a manager to assist in in the day to day tasks. I must admit feeling more than overwhelmed. However, their true intentions soon became vividly clear.

Mrs. Clairabel Fitzpatrick, as cunning as she is sweet, made arrangements for tea and I felt I should meet with her. After All, Mother always insisted good manners and a kind demeanor are the most valuable traits a lady can possess. So, we met and she told me about the organization, presented me with a formal invitation to join and, I believe to gain my trust or perhaps to befriend me, she imparted some advice about employing management.

Naturally, Mr. Baker had already suggested I do this very thing. I told Mrs. Fitzpatrick so. From there we discussed many different aspects of business and such before finally ending the engagement. I found her amusing and did suggest that if she knew anyone who could work at such a task, then to please send them to me.

So, before I knew it, I had woman after woman lined up at my office. Each more progressive than the last. I turned the whole matter oven to Mr. Baker. He, in the end, made the brilliant suggestion of hiring a man. Who better to communicate with other men?

I am not interested in furthering someone else's politics. I do not, nor ever have I wished to lead some progressive movement. Thus is a grandeur more befitting Arthur's mother than myself. Perhaps that is all she has left to fill her days. I, however, am filled to the brim and would simply appreciate anyone who can get everything accomplished. It just to happens, that right now, that usually requires a gentleman rather than a business lady.

Perhaps someday in the future, life may not be so. But alas, for now I would prefer investments that grow rather to forging history. Mr. Baker said, "Now that is the way a man thinks."

I know he meant to compliment me, so I took no offense. Though I still find it difficult to believe any such words spoken about me. I fear I may soon cease to blush at such comments. But so many of the businesses I hold a partnership in are run by men who talk to me as they would placate a daughter with a silly, but harmless, hobby. They do not take me seriously. In hopes of prosperous business, I now have Peter and he they will respect.

Perhaps I should have done this ages ago, yet then I would never have learned my own ability. I wanted to try for Father's sake. Though I wished Arthur to have it all. Since he did not desire to help, a part of me wanted to prove to him that I am more than a spoiled woman who can think of nothing more distressful than the pattern of lace I'd prefer on my new dress. Perhaps there was a time that was so, but no more. I also did not quite understand the theory of delegating responsibility.

I feel nothing like I used to. The world and my life are much different than I thought. It is nothing like the daydreams of a child. How many times have I said that over the years? I miss Mother and Father. However, I am ever so thankful for you. Please remember to tell me how my dear aunt and uncle are doing. Now that Father has passed, I fear I shall never see them again. And your sister, please give her my love.

I hope to hear from you soon. If only the post could speed as far as our hearts would let them. Please take diligent care of yourself and give Carlita the sweetest of kisses from me.

Very truly yours,
Maggie

19 September, 1902

Dear Cousin Rachel,

I received your letter and my heart leapt with excitement Another child, how envious I feel. Although I am concerned for your health, I know you have accomplished much, already. I have no need to sit and worry as I do, sometimes. Perhaps I can make a trip of it and visit you soon. Yet I cannot help but feel there is something more you wish to say, as though some secret lingers about, hidden behind what you write. Though now that I think of it: it has been there a long time. I have been so consumed with my own life, I've failed to notice. So, I must ask you to trust me. I fear you have been a much kinder friend than I. In your letter, you mentioned a girl named Adora , such a lovely name, but I cannot recall her. Yet you seem to know her quite well. I am sorry she has caused you grief, but it sounds as though you love her very much. Is she a niece of your husband's? Does she live with you? How old is she? Artie has already begun his age of tantrums. She sounds older though. I found it peculiar that she should be envious of the baby and angry about the news of another one soon, But I am not accustomed to Mexican traditions or their family way. Perhaps such things are natural. I know little Artie might feel overwhelmed with jealousy should we have another child. Though I cannot foresee such a thing happening. No, it seems my little darling is the only motherly blessing I shall receive. But think not that I am bitter for that. I have far too many wonderful things in my life to dwell upon the disappointments.

Yes, I have clearly thought long about my life and what it means. I felt so sure that God must have been angry with me, that perhaps I had claimed some terrible punishment for sins I could not fathom. The loss of Mother, then Father's marriage to that wretched woman, the loss of father and then the shocking betrayal of my husband. Even this does not give justice to the turmoil I suffered. But then I look at all the blessings as well and the incredible journey my life has become. I have still so much to learn. Fear clutches my heart sometimes, albeit, now I can see past the fear and know that all will be well.

Of course, life is only that. Nothing more than life. It is a sequence of tragedies written across the pages of books where beauty waxes through, dancing to the drumming beat of our heart. While you can see someone's idle dance, you can never hear the rise a fall of the music that plays only to ones self. This is what I have decided regarding life.

Now that I have said this, there is a confession I must utter, I cannot disclose it to anyone here, certainly, for no one knows the situation. And recent conversations which I shall impart leave my conscience in a delicate quandary.

Arthur and I spoke at length a fortnight past. I have come to a better understanding of his condition, I call it thus for good reason. It seems he has always, for as long as he can recall, been afflicted such. He claims that at a very young age, his mother sensed a problem and worked diligently his whole life to both correct and disguise what she called his ailment.

At first, this revelation surprised me. I felt truly deceived and then my thoughts turned to my own worries for little Artie and my own intentions to secure his future. At that point, my hurt and anger dissolved into empathy. I know exactly how she felt. I understand the fear for your child that grips around the bosom and squeezes the breath from your lungs. She wanted to avoid for him a life shamed by others.

What broke my heart though was the realization that my husband could never truly love me the way I hoped. A part of me wanted to believe that he merely harbored some ill perversion that such an act could satisfy, but the truth is that the ailment resides not in his loins but in his heart. I can never give him the love he desires, either. We are both trapped as such, though it seems he has been a captive his whole life.

Arthur says there are many like him and they all live in secret, unable to disclose their nature for fear of losing everything they have and disgracing their families. He does not know if his tendency is an illness or a product of nature, but because it is a sin in the Church, no one dares to make confrontations over it.

But Arthur does care for me. He loves me in the only fashion he can. He hates that I feel prey to his mother's schemes but takes responsibility for it. And after all, he should. For I did not court his mother, though he says that she specifically chose me as his match. He said she underestimated my intellect.

But here is where my quandary begins. You see, Arthur divulged that he simply did not feel he could perform the duties of a husband and reciprocate the affections I wished to give. He also explained that through no fault of mine, I could never fill the void in his heart. He did not wish to divorce, for such a thing would help no one and would certainly end his political hopes. He suggested that we maintain a public marriage while pursuing discrete relationships with more appropriate lovers.

I told him I needed some time to consider such a proposal. There are many concerns I have with this, not the least of which, my soul being condemned to eternal damnation for adultery. But is it adultery if your husband is unable to be such?

This would not be nearly so difficult a decision if not for an additional dilemma. It appears that Mr. Floyd, the gentlemen I mentioned before, whom I hired as my Manager of Affairs, wishes to manage more than business. He has expressed interest in me that seems rather inappropriate. I brought the situation to Arthur. Childish really, but I fear my heart prayed for a jealous outrage, one that shook him into a violent outburst and thus curing his ailment. But perhaps, even knowing the end, my heart so longed to hear him protest. Become angry. I needed some boundary too cross and know that he would fight to keep me. What girl does not sit and conjure fanciful plans about a handsome beast? Well, by beast, I mean a powerful man who lives without want, or need until, like the first flower of Spring, he sees her, set ablaze by the rising sun, she cascades in a fiery approach across glittering petals ,soft as velvet. Every woman wants to be that irresistible flower, the one he cannot fathom life without. As old as I have become; it appears, I am still nothing more than a child. In my zeal for love and impatience for marriage, I too believed in fairly tales. And even now, when I know all is lost, here I find myself once more, thinking, wishing, pleading that perhaps, by some miracle I can change my husband to a man who wants me.

What is more, I want him to become outraged and furious. I know those emotions are buried deep within him. Why can't he feel them for me?

I believe I would rather have married a philanderer. At least then I could understand. But when I brought the issue of Mr. Floyd to his attention, I wanted my husband to explode with jealousy at the mere thought of another man's arms slipping around my waist, then pulling my body close to his. I wanted passion: yet what did I receive for all my efforts? A sudden fit of jealousy? Fury enough to cure his ailment? No. His face lit up and he took my hands, leading me to the settee. I followed, not sure if wrath would soon emerge. But he then did what I could never prepared myself for. Arthur, my husband, began to speak. And his words, you will not believe it and I pray you burn this letter before it ever has the chance to be read by anyone else.

Once seated, he began asking questions more likened to a school girl than a jealous husband. or lover. He wanted to know all about Mr. Floyd. Even asked me to invite him to dinner one evening. He thought it wonderful that I had so quickly found a lover. He even complimented me, saying that I am such a lovely woman, beautiful and graceful.

He did say that if any woman in the world could ever hold his heart, he knew it would be me.

He then made plans for Mr. Floyd and myself. Arthur feels that long term relationships will provide the safest situation and that, at some point, in order to maintain honesty, I will have to tell him the reason behind our deception.

Far from the violent anger I had built myself up to withstand, and I know, finally, I know, that Arthur and I have a marriage. in law only. I feel sure I will never have anything more with him. Why did I have to rush myself? It would be so easy to blame that meddling step mother who kept on and on interfering with everything, Her saying I shouldn't have something only made it worse. And if the Rutherfords are such a fine and elite family, how could they stand by and allow something so horrible happen? How could they let me marry him? Why not his brother. At least I know he favors women, a scoundrel though he be.

Well, here I am, ranting once more. Before long you shall say, "oh, look. A letter from my poor cousin, she has been touched for some years now."

I fear I may already have earned the honor!

But in the end, all my fantasies aside, Arthur encouraged me to see Mr. Floyd at least once. He knows that I need such company and says no true harm could come of it, so long as outings are properly planned. I still do not know what to do. I feel as though my soul hangs in balance, yet it teeters to and fro.

Now I believe I have said all there is to tell. I am so happy for you. What I would not give for another child.

I had best end here. I love you so much Rachel. I envy both your strength and love. They are worth everything. Bless you and your family, and especially your children. If ever you need time to spare, feel free to lend them to me for a while. I think they would enjoy it here. All my love to you.

Love Always,
Maggie

14 November, 1902

Dearest Cousin Rachel,

My dear. I am so sorry. At first, upon reading your letter, I could not understand why you kept this from me and for so long. I admit my heart ached. I did not understand why you did not trust me. But once I reflected on the past years and thought of all that has occurred, I realized how easily you would feel the need to hide this. After all, were I in your place, I fear I could not allow your defense of me to end in your broken heart. For I surely would have confronted both Arthur and Jonathan. To think that I once thought him a suitable match for you. It is so difficult to believe that a family like his could be so heartless and cruel, but now that I have been part of that family, I have learned just how vicious they truly are.

You know that he did marry a few months ago, I had not mentioned this because I knew you did not care for him. I have never forgotten what you wrote long ago. Even then I suspected some sort of deceit, but I would never have guessed the truth.

A lady must beware any man who claims any cause to suit her in secret. His fear of your father was merely a rouse to take advantage of a love struck girl. These Rutherfords are filled with deceit down to the core of their souls. To see what they even do to one another.

Oh, and I think of that smart little girl he married. She has the audacity to belittle me. I have ignored her because, in honesty, I felt her a trifle in comparison to my other concerns. She comes from little better than nothing. She has no education or wealth. She is merely a pretty face.

And it appears that Arthur's parents have decided he may be ill prepared to seek a political future. I heard him arguing with his father about it a week ago in the library. They believe that Jonathan is better equipped for such a venture. That is the idea behind his marriage. I wonder if she knows that scoundrel only married her because she has a pretty face and his family thinks that a common wife will lend him sympathy among less fortunate voters. She is a pawn in Mr. Rutherford's pursuit of power.

Though I am not one to judge her in this. Who has been a greater fool than I? But even still, for the sake of grace, whom could ever believe you would lie about such a thing. It is so unfair. He is allowed his scandalous reputation and men shake his hand and their heads at the same time, finding it all in good fun. As they do so, you, as beautiful and wonderful a young lady as there could ever be, you are ridiculed and shunned. I am so sorry. I feel somehow I should have been a better friend. Is there anything I can do?

Oh my! I have only just thought of how difficult it must have been for you out West, living on a ranch without friends or anyone. You family is truly wonderful. It is amazing how Uncle Theodore left everything behind to save you from humiliation. I wish I had known about your daughter all this time. I would have loved sending her gifts. It is wrong that you should suffer so when he bares nothing of shame or responsibility. You are better than he ever deserved. Feel better in knowing this, you have a wonderful husband who loves and worships you while that loathsome vermin spends the rest of this existence tied to a silly girl with naught for intelligence. I am quite sure his mother is desperately bothered that her new daughter in law is from common lineage. She prides herself so in her family's heritage. All the while, you are married to a prince of men and the whole of town is in a flutter of jealousy. Perhaps they underestimated how much you are loved. I believe anyone can be a valuable member of our community. Look what I have accomplished.

Your husband is truly a priceless gem among men, knowing of your daughter and willing to raise her as his own. That is such a wonderful and admirable quality in a man. It is no wonder you love his so.

Now I have delayed answering your question as long as possible. No. I have not accepted Mr. Floyd's flirtations. However, I have not denied him either. Arthur's words stung my heart, yet I cannot deny the truth he spoke. While Mr. Floyd seems a respectable man, I must question the honor of one so willing to begin an affair with a married lady. Is my heart destined to only loneliness unless

to place your money is the same as buying quality fabrics or fine lace. I simply applied the same standards of quality and the choices become clear. But do not tell anyone. The men laugh at me enough as it is.

Never forget you are a beautiful lady. So many wrongs have cluttered your life and it is unjust. Feel content in your love for your family, for life is truly lost without them. What are riches if there is only yourself to bestow them upon?

Give my love to all.

Very truly yours,
Maggie

CHAPTER SIX: 1903

My Dear Cousin Rachel,

   Sweet Rachel, how could I ever hold you in anything but the highest esteem. I cannot blame you for such a deception. I have learned too well that women, ladies or not, do as they must to survive. I shall never say a word to anyone. How could I? My own life is a labyrinth of deceit. You have only done as needed to give both your daughter and yourself a happy and fortunate future. While I fear she may be cheated her rightful inheritance, sparing her the shame and pain of abandonment by her father is truly more valuable than the sum of any fortune. There is no shame in the death of ones parent. At least the Rutherfords did make some compensation for their son's wicked manner.

   And so I have said what my heart feels, I do not want you to carry on or worry about it any longer. Your confidence heals many wounds. Not to say that were inflicted by you, for they were not. But to know that life is neither simple nor wholly blessed I and that you trust me with the most secret confessions hidden from all else but God, that is what warms my soul and gives me hope.

Only five years has passed since you journeyed West to meet your fate with your family. Life has changed for us both in ways we could never dared to believe. So much is gone that once filled our hearts and minds with tender and innocent joy. While tragedies have stalked our days since parted, still much is new that while sometimes bittersweet, radiates enough happiness and hope to make every tear only a passing storm. I feel hope where only a short time go, I felt none.

I did speak with the Father on the day of my last letter. I pondered long upon his words and advice. He left me with many things to consider-I fear my belief in the Church waivered for a time.

As I am sure you knew from the moment you read my idea, it is impossible to obtain an annulment in such a circumstance, as we already have a son. However, it appears that the Father already knows or suspects the true nature of my dilemma. For he chose his words carefully.

I spoke with Father Philippe who has been here only a few years after missionary work abroad. He told me that should Arthur admit to the Church that he married me falsely and be willing to both confess the nature of his sin and withdraw from the Church, then the Church will allow a divorce by law and the status of a widow.

There were other suggestions, but those were similar to now. My heart simply cannot continue in a constant lie. It is times such as these when I miss Mother the most. I believe she would know the answer. Oh my, yes. I have forgotten the crown. Such forgiveness is certainly attainable with a generous donation. Our tithe alone cannot make adequate amends. It is this that struck my heart as a dagger. I must first convince my husband to admit his deviance and agree to leave the Church forever and then forgiveness and freedom is mine for a price. I nearly called him a carpetbagger when I finally understood his meaning.

And then yet, what also is there? I can never be happy

in my marriage. I here also discovered that my conscience cannot cross the boundaries of marriage into adultery. I admit that I tried to open myself to Mr. Floyd's affection, but to no avail. I could perhaps care for him. As queer as it may sound, that seems to be the very reason I cannot follow a path of deceit. I see in his eyes that he knows my marriage is not real, Though I do not believe he suspects the truth of it all. It may be a fanciful dream, but I sometimes think what it might be to share my life with him. He is thoughtful and kind. He certainly knows all of the business, so I could return to managing the household. I cannot deny that doing both is sometimes overwhelming and I feel the faint approaching. Were it not for such wonderful ladies to help me, I could never do it all. And I had Father's home to keep as well. Arthur tells me I should sell our family estate. He does not think I need the added worries. But I could never do such a thing. Could you imagine my doing so? Father would fall from heaven and haunt me the rest of my days. And anyway, I feel safe there. This mansion is so large, the hallways echo with the sounds of footsteps. I sometimes lay in bed at night listening to others scuttle about and think this must be what it is like to live in a castle. The vast emptiness here sometimes scares me. I wish to be neither a princess nor a queen. A wife and mother should be well enough for me.

Yes. I know what you would say if you were here. First, you would chastise me for not doing what is so obvious. I shall. I promise to speak with Arthur. Father Philippe assured me that Arthur's confession would be discreet and in confidence. He would be free to tell what he wished about leaving the Church. And in truth, I do still love him very much. My heart aches for him as well. He cannot find love or happiness so long as he remains bound to me or to the Church. I fear for his soul, but since he cannot change the way of his self, no more than I could become a bird, then I must accept the perfect ideal of God. He made Arthur as he is for a purpose. I do not understand it, but there is much in this world beyond my feeble ability to grasp.

I so wish you could come for a holiday. I realize your condition does not permit such travels. It is merely the longing of my heart to see an old friend. Perhaps I should consider a holiday somewhere. Maybe abroad. How I wish I could be more like you. I am unsure what enchantment binds me here. The thought of sailing away to the old world both terrifies and thrills me. Yet even as I daydream, I know it is nothing more. How could I leave everything my father built? Could I abandon the treasurer he entrusted to me?

Rachel, so much has changed for me in these last years. I have grown in ways I never understood possible. To speak the truth, I have become someone I never knew I would want to be. While I know that everyone thinks I am a spoiled woman, the truth is that I am afraid. I spend every day so terrified of making a mistake. How I wish father had better prepared me for this responsibility The Herald writes about me all the time. It seems I have become a second past time, The society page is full of nosey commentary on my life. I have one half of the women in town saying how wonderful I am, "A real inspiration." While the others think I am an abomination. It is a constant bombardment of praise and scorn. I have no wish be a leader for women. I do not know the answers for women's rights.

I do not believe Father intended so much be thrust upon me. Father wanted my happiness more than anything. Perhaps that is my answer to all these queries in any heart. What would Father expect and want for me and little Artie?

I must end here. Please know that I will keep your secret forever. I hate that it must be so for you, but understand the necessity. I have a few things to which I must attend. I believe I have a bargain to conduct.

Please send my love to Uncle Theodore and the rest,

give your precious daughters kisses each from me. I have enclosed a small gift for them. I love you all and pray to see you soon. Keep in good health.

Very truly yours,
Maggie

30 March, 1903

Dearest Cousin Rachel,

Please forgive how long it has taken me to return your post. I have had much to do. I fear I have had Mr. Baker in a bit of a state. Truly, I have you to thank. While writing my last letter to you, a sudden realization came upon me. Father always wanted nothing more or less than my true happiness. He was a man of his own record, not abiding to the wishes and whims of others. What other man would have left such a fortune to a spoiled daughter? And remember his intent to have me schooled right here when all else insisted that I should the sent away to school? He did not ever follow the lead of others. I believe I would make him most proud if I followed his example. I have chosen to be my father's daughter, but oddly, it is not the path I first thought.

Oh Rachel, I made a terrible mistake. I thought I had to become successful in Father's businesses to make him proud of me. I forsake myself and what he and Mother taught me. I believe father knew, or at the very least, suspected that Arthur's affection was disingenuous. He bequeathed his fortune to me, a lifetime of work, to insure a means for my happiness. I lost myself trying to earn the trust he showed. But as it turned, I became shrewd enough to survive.

Look at my explaining. Best now to move forward. I have made some changes. Little Artie and I have purchased passage to London, where I intend to spend the next year. It shall be an extended holiday while the ugly

happiness. If that means someone else, so be it. Perhaps now that he has seen someone confront his father, a woman no less, and win, he may now become more confident and independent.

Of it all, what hurt the most, was that Mr. and Mrs. Rutherford revealed no desire to see little Artie. This saddens me, as my parents are gone. He deserves so much better.

This seems to be all there is to tell. Arthur will keep this estate. I have been packaging all mine and little Artie's things. They shall be railed to Baltimore. I have a last fitting for a strolling dress at Lovell's today. I needed something more appropriate for the voyage. It should take seven days to cross over to London. I do hope the sickness does not take me, but I am sure Artie will do fine. He still loves to be rocked

I will have Mr. Baker send you the new post when it is sorted and I am prepared to receive.

Thank you, Rachel. You have been the very best of friends and family. You are as nearest a sister as one could ever have. I love you so much. Please give well wishes to your family. I will send the children presents from Europe. Please rest and keep your health. I hope to write again soon, perhaps while we cross the great ocean.

All my love,
Maggie

.

Here ends the story of Margaret Florence Baine. To discover the stories of more women in the Letters' Series visit the author's website at www.AnnLavendar.com

Or for these and additional books available from

LeeLoo Publishing™ visit
http://leeloopub.bravesites.com/

ABOUT THE AUTHOR

Ann Lavendar lives in the beautiful mountains of Southern California with her husband, Jake, her youngest son, Woodrow, two dogs and three cats.
Learn more about Ann Lavendar, her other books and stories, public events and upcoming releases by visiting her website.
http://AnnLavendar.com

www.ingramcontent.com/pod-product-compliance
Lightning Source LLC
Chambersburg PA
CBHW030639130626

46552CB00002B/922